Liz Heron grew up in Scotland [...] University. She lived in Paris [...] settling in London in 1976 [...] publications as a literary and photographic critic and has trans-lated novels, short stories, criticism and philosophy by French and Italian authors. Her previous books are *Changes of Heart* (1986) and, as editor, *Truth, Dare or Promise* (Virago 1985, 1993), *Streets of Desire* (Virago 1993) and *Illuminations: Women Writing on Photography from the 1850s to the Present* (1996, co-edited with Val Williams). This is her first work of fiction.

A RED RIVER

Liz Heron

A *Virago* Book

First published in Great Britain
in 1996 by Virago Press

A CIP catalogue record for this book is
available from the British Library.

ISBN 1 85381 869 0

Typeset in Bembo by M Rules
Printed and bound in Great Britain by
Clays Ltd, St Ives plc

Virago
A Division of
Little, Brown and Company (UK)
Brettenham House
Lancaster Place
London WC2E 7EN

For M. J. I.

Contents

A Red River

They marry in May, on a perfect cloudless morning. Birdsong woke Joseph at dawn, after too few hours of dreamful, sweat-ridden sleep; dreams of his father and his long-dead mother . . . Which solitary bird sang so loudly at his window on the morning of his wedding? He should have asked Andrés. It nagged him not to know.

Stepping down on the springy grass outside the church he becomes aware of wingbeats overhead. More late swallows relishing a landfall, wheeling towards the tower, settling there, then gliding off westwards and further up the estuary. This joyful sight will be a true clear omen to remember for his children, and his anxious mind at once releases that nameless songbird from his faint irritation with it.

By the time she arrives he is calm and cooler, feeling almost that he has charmed himself into serenity, as he is wont to charm others. The morning coat seems a better fit now, and there is no haste in the tick of his father's watch as it nestles in the silk of his deepest waistcoat pocket. He stands as he has pictured himself at this moment, an eager ardent bridegroom.

Watching Pilar walk towards him at the altar he knows his most intense emotion to be pride. Pride not only in her beauty, which stuns him once more with its radiance, but the pride of his own achievement at marrying this woman of his choice against all the odds. Pride is what he has always been warned against, but who could separate it now from the pure glow of happiness which illumines the two of them?

'Do you, Joseph Alexander Finlay, take this woman . . .?'

'Do you, María del Pilar de Breda y Gutiérrez Blanco . . .?'

At Pilar's silent prompting, Joseph kneels and their hands touch briefly in a flush of secrecy among the rich satin folds of her dress. She bows her head in prayer. He turns, gazing at her profile: the full sensual mouth, the long lowered lashes, the pale olive brow swept clear, the curls caught under high combs and cascading white lace. He turns away, in sudden embarrassment at his look being remarked by the many pairs of curious eyes behind them. He too assumes an attitude of prayer, although religious feeling is not in his nature. This had made it easier to exchange one religion for another.

Joseph Finlay is a Scot, a Presbyterian by upbringing, and in order to marry Pilar he has taken religious instruction. The Catholic Church received him as a convert a month before the wedding. He was glad of the prompt decision to hold the ceremony at Los Robles, a common enough arrangement for a family of this standing. But Pilar was dismayed by the news. She was fond of the church at Moguer and had imagined being married there rather than at home. Joseph could not bear to see her disappointment and gave way. Doña Cristina was persuaded, inclined on this occasion to indulge her grand-daughter. So it turned out that the wedding, already the talk of the district, was destined to be a truly public spectacle. And indeed, the church overflows, while outside in the sunshine a waiting crowd looks on as the couple appear.

Some wish them well, others simply stare. They are women for the most part, but Joseph wonders how so many had the leisure to idle, on this, a working day.

Without thinking, he had scanned the faces in the church for Matheson's, while knowing full well that he would never set foot inside a den of Papists; nor was he likely to join their wedding celebrations, though as it happened he was now in Spain, due on special business down in Huelva. A handsome set of crystal had been sent, and a letter, albeit a curt one, wishing Joseph well in the fulfilment of his matrimonial duties and expressing the hope that with God's help he might bring the word of Grace to his future wife. Joseph had laughed when he read this. But it was still a triumph, when he had thought that Matheson would shun him, for all the ties of family friendship. Had his father played a part?

They drive out of Moguer, a carillon at their backs, in a creamy blur of petals whirling through the blue air, as the younger guests, armed with freshly picked roses and jasmine and yellow carnations, set upon their landau, which is already decorated with blooms. At intervals hands reach out from a window above and unleash yet another scented storm. And then, on the road, the fragrance of the peach orchards hazes over them.

It is nearly noon. The drive to the estate takes an hour at normal pace, but the newlyweds, heading a procession of carriages and single riders, are waylaid and sometimes have to stop as the latter canter up to them to wish them well again and shed more petals on their heads. Once or twice they are hailed by women weeding in the grain fields and Pilar asks Roque to rein in the horses so that she can see who they are and call out to them by name. Pilar laughs a lot at these encounters and is more girlish than Joseph has ever seen her, more spontaneous, less self-conscious that is, at last oblivious to propriety. This is the melting, softening core he looks for when he kisses her, which he does whenever the landau puts the others at a distance, and at other times besides. Does she merely yield to him more or is there some other alteration under way? Are not young unmarried women compelled to walk a tightrope of decorum? Pilar is eighteen, he will be thirty in less than a month. He has courted other women half-seriously long before he knew her; he has even had a mistress, but he has never had a bride. He watches her laughter, hears her shouts to riders and their mounts, all of whom she knows and seems to want beside her in the gaiety of this journey. He is stirred by this thought of a young virgin woman changing into his wife, her feet on strange untrodden ground, but terra firma all the same.

As they drive up into Los Robles, Pilar seems to sober a little.

They are fifty at the long oak tables shaded by rush awnings and the branches of fruit trees, almond and flowering plum, quince and persimmon. The servants have a trestle of their own set up behind the barn and even those attending them at table become a little tipsy as the afternoon goes on.

This feast has a local abundance from the mountains and the sea: sole and shrimps and baked tunny-fish, succulent Jabugo hams and plump *salsichones*, spit-roast lamb, larks in wine sauce and wild asparagus, and the sherry from Doña Cristina's own vines. Only the champagne which Joseph had ordered from the Huelva shippers has come from outside the province. As food is brought to him so are guests – by the priests and Doña Cristina and his friend and best man Andrés Padilla; he meets those of the district's gentry that are not already of his acquaintance. Then there are the relatives from Seville and many others, some clearly a little in awe of him and this, his bridal conquest: that Pilar should marry an *inglés*. For, however much he and his compatriots contradict this slight on nationality with furious assertions of their provenance, in the eyes of those that Matheson and his ilk call 'the natives', they are members of the *English* colony.

And it is Matheson who provides the afternoon's surprise.

With only Eddie Ewart there as ballast for the Scot in him, Joseph has wellnigh surrendered the ties of Caledonia to Andalusia, on the verge of forgetting who he is, which is to say not a Spaniard. He imagines too in some part of his usually sharp brain, now drunk with nuptial euphoria and alcohol, that by marrying Pilar he is achieving a peace between two warring nations, a calculated love-match rather than a reckless one. Then, like some wizard in a fairy-tale, Matheson turns up, on his way from Huelva to Río Tinto, having left the train to meet the British Consul who is on a local visit about export papers. They drive up unnoticed by Joseph and have to be announced; a hush descends as people turn to look at them.

'I'm much honoured, sir.' Joseph tries to clear his head, longing now for strong black coffee.

The Consul accepts a *manzanilla*, Matheson a cordial, the courtesies demanded by the occasion are exchanged and then the two men are gone in a matter of ten minutes, less time than it takes for the atmosphere they leave behind to be dispelled. More than one member of the wedding party has wished Matheson in hell.

He kisses her shoulder, then slides a fingertip over the hollow of her neck, drawing his hand down on to her shuddering belly. Except for his wedding gift, the diamond necklace which Pilar still wears, they are both naked now; he has wanted to devote himself to her pleasure, and hours have gone by. He kisses her thighs and spreads one hand tight across her collarbone in a caress that encompasses the diamonds. He whispers to her: '*Mi amor.*' He adores her.

She feels herself smile, the smile fills her eyes and as her eyes close and her neck arches back on the pillow she feels helpless, a prolonged delightful helplessness; but for the gasps and shudders and spasms he induces in her she cannot move – her body has no will of its own. She can no longer tell which part of her is being stroked or kissed or held or pressed. Sensation wells through her like wine.

Something scuttles on the balcony: a mouse perhaps, and she remembers the dream she woke with that morning. A dream about the moon, high and full above the oak wood that her bedroom overlooks, and hares that run in pursuit of the female through the undergrowth, their blood pounding, the almost silent pad of hunters' feet behind them. A dream which had given her a little jolt of guilt or shame, she can scarcely think which, that same morning, now a long time ago.

The Company

The Company bought the mines in 1873 for the sum of £3,680,000 – on condition they be ceded in perpetuity and with no right to royalties for the Spanish state. An old Spanish story, of bankruptcies and borrowings and bargains. Matheson's bargain: Europe's richest and most extensive cupreous deposits – a truly copper-bottomed one it must have seemed to this canny Scotsman – had to be backed by substantial funds for developing the mines, for building a railway, bridges, the pier at Huelva. Investment on a scale beyond Spanish means.

Finance sources were many and varied, banks mostly, in Scotland and England, but foreign capital played a part too. An initial triumvirate supplying the purchase price was formed by Matheson's own London merchant house, along with the railway construction firm of Clark, Punchard and Co., and the Deutsche National Bank of Bremen. The progress of the operation might have been jeopardised had the subsequent challenge to the Matheson prospectus been successful. Tharsis, a Glasgow-based venture with mine workings to the west of Río Tinto (and where the French had earlier had a concession), watched with growing alarm as the project's scope was revealed and they saw the newcomer's potential for underselling them on the copper and pyrites market. The railway was built, the pier completed, and Tharsis still poured public doubts upon the wisdom of investment. Matheson countered with the Deby Report, commissioned by the Company in 1878. It exaggerated ore reserves. The shareholders were duly reassured, and, for all the report's downright inaccuracy (the writer had, in mitigation, no first-hand knowledge, never having seen the mines) they did well to have faith in the Company, which in the fullness of time paid them very handsome dividends. As for opposition from the Spanish, the local elite had at first no objection to the Company's presence, for it doled out the expected liberal gratuities to *caciques* and bureaucrats. Expansion and consolidation followed. By the start of the 1880s the Company had become Spain's largest single employer. By April 1885 it had complete control of public services in the mining district, an area including the towns of Río Tinto, Nerva and Zalamea; and at Río Tinto the town hall itself was Company property. It is now 1887: the Company truly rules, but things stir in its kingdom and down among its subjects.

Pilar asks Joseph if he will take her to the mines. The request surprises him. He says no, curtly, planting a dismissive kiss on her brow; then, as a guilty afterthought, he smiles, his eyes shifting into a gentler focus, holding hers with full attention, and he asks her why she would want to do such a thing, to go where there would be nothing but dirt and dust and rough, loudmouthed miners who breathe *aguardiente* and onion.

'Because you work there, you spend your days there, and I am here, trying to imagine it. Also because I want to see things for myself, however much you tell me.'

'How wayward you are, my girl.' He laughs.

Marriage has moderated Pilar's shy gravity and her frivolous-
ness — for her temperament, as Joseph has observed, swung
between the two. It is now finding a balance that pleases him.
This might suggest that Pilar's was an unformed personality.
But though she lacked maturity, she did not altogether lack
knowledge of the world. She was not uneducated and had the
advantage of growing up in a household where, contrary to all
custom, women ruled. And these two facts are, of course,
connected. She was not packed off to the nuns at an early age
but remained at home with her grandmother, who had too
much fondness for the orphaned child to let her go so young.
Her first tutor, the curate Don Alfonso, grateful enough to
find a quick and eager mind, having had his fill of dullards, for
much of the time forgot she was a girl. It was he who taught
her to read and write, as well as a little Greek and quite a lot
of Latin, through dogged translation of Virgil and Cicero, and
guided her study of the gospels.

At twelve she was sent to Seville to learn to be a proper
señorita. There she stayed at the house of her aunt Enriqueta,
her mother's younger sister, and with her cousins Lola and
Luisa became a pupil at the French Academy for young ladies.
Shortly before her sixteenth birthday she returned to Los
Robles, having acquired excellent French, a smattering of
English and a taste for reading foreign novels. Her music
lessons had equipped her with a pleasant, tuneful, though
sometimes tremulous voice, and average competence at the
piano. Now, her formal education ceased, with the exception
of the latter activity, since twice a week Madame Renault, a

widowed relic from the days of the French concession, the Compagnie des Mines de Cuivres d'Huelva, would arrive from Moguer to put her through her musical paces. Usually, being on friendly terms with Doña Cristina, Madame would stay to lunch and Pilar would drink in the gossip to which the music teacher's peripatetic family intimacies gave her access. As a child, Pilar had been frail and rather timid – which had been forgiven in her orphaned state. But this meant she had little inclination for riding, something which provoked general astonishment in view of her grandmother's own equestrian skills. To this day she rode little, though she liked to watch others on horseback and was happy enough at the reins of a gig or a dog cart. It was remarked that she was more reflective than other girls of her age, even a trifle moody, and by the time she and Joseph met she had already refused two offers of marriage that would have been perfectly acceptable to her family.

Joseph is fond of recalling one detail of their meeting. This had been at the house of Andrés Padilla, a young fellow of no profession but ample inherited means, a sometime poet and painter, a little dandified with his groomed goatee and dapper elegance: a ladies' man. His Sunday afternoon teas *a la inglesa*, at which a great deal of sherry was drunk, were his way of reiterating to the world that he had not the slightest interest in boar hunting, nor hunting of any other kind for that matter, the most common male pastime of that sacred day in those parts.

What Joseph recalls are Pilar's green stockings, her ankles being what drew his eyes when he had entered the drawing-room and seen her on a long blue rep sofa listening to a conversation between her grandmother and Andrés. He then noticed that both her hat and her grey silk dress were trimmed with the same sage green. Pilar could never understand why he thought green stockings were racy.

'Oh, but you were the picture of girlish modesty!' he would say.

He had known very well, after six months at the colony, that it was not the done thing to consort with Spanish girls. Andrés' teas *a la inglesa* were plainly not in honour of the English, who never attended (the Scots likewise); this absence, whether by refusal or exclusion, was their very attraction for Joseph and made him feel especially favoured by the friendship of the host. The not-done thing did not deter him. On the contrary, he had had in mind to find himself a Spanish mistress. Joseph, the man of the world, the smudge-blonde, blue-eyed angel, erstwhile Lothario of Pollokshields and Kelvinside, had decided long since that he was in thrall to Mediterranean women. At twenty-three he had embarked on his first real sexual adventure, with a smartly-dressed young milliner in Leghorn, having sailed there to begin a tour of Italy. Instead, he had stayed for more than six weeks, spending each night with the sad-eyed Luciana, who knew he would leave her in the end. This passion was decisive in his notion of himself as too much a European to feel at home elsewhere. Despite an attractive offer that came via his father, the South African diamond fields held no lure for him at all. They would have been a banishment to some truly nether world of mineral darkness – one too far flung from everything he knew, and he was well aware he lacked the instinct of the conquering pioneer.

For all his father's surprise at the refusal, it had then seemed quite natural to the old man that Joseph should work for Matheson in Spain and this was smoothly arranged. Hector Finlay had known the chairman since their boyhood in Edinburgh and each had helped the other. In '72 he had accompanied Matheson to Persia as consultant on a survey for the Reuter's concession, but the whole venture had been thwarted when the Shah got cold feet and wanted his country back. Río Tinto was maybe Persia as it would have been in miniature: the Company mines spawned a Company railway, and Company houses and a Company school, and, for the Company's staff, a hilltop enclave with those tall gabled villas and a clubhouse, a polo ground and cricket pitch behind well-guarded gates. Río Tinto was, indeed, another outpost of Empire. But with less local inconvenience as far as Joseph was concerned, and more means of escape from the narrowness of a colony.

This narrowness, believes Joseph, derives in part from education, and he is sure, as Scots so often are, that his own itinerary through learning took him down byways of knowledge and experience that would forever be unknown to his English colleagues, formed as they were by the self-enclosing culture of the suburbs and the public school. Since the age of eight his schooling had been conventional enough for Scotland and his class, but more open to the world than anything Sassenach. There had been a tutor, the Grammar, then Glasgow University. At seven, in the year after his mother's death, when they had sent him to stay with her sister, he attended the school at Kilmaurs: the village school where the Dominie ruled with an even-handed tyranny of tawse and tongue over a motley of the poor and rural well-to-do.

Joseph believes too in his own enlightenment, which scorns his compatriots in Calvin and Knox, their apparent belief that God could be duped by outward show, their sheeplike obedience to every edict by the General Manager, whom they seemed to regard as Matheson's representative on Earth; the way that Catholics see the Pope as a ventriloquist's doll for the Almighty. This uncouth comparison would be deemed a Papist blasphemy, of course; in the days before the chaplain's coming, when the great man himself preached hellfire sermons two hours long and attendance obligatory, His Holiness was but the anti-Christ.

So many things prompted Joseph to fall in love with Pilar . . .

She, like him, was an only child, and like him had lost her mother – indeed both parents – at an early age. They died on a ship that went down on the crossing to Cuba, the country of her father's origin, when she was four. Joseph was stricken when he heard this, though it was not from Pilar's own lips. No more total loss could he imagine than a beloved body cast to the depths of the ocean. No corpse, no grave, no proof of death that could be touched. Just absence, perpetual. The heartache of it made him tender.

After meeting her for the second time, and only briefly, he wrote to his father, for he knew it would be difficult at first and he had to make a start, the strategy a gradual wearing down of prejudices.

> *My dear father,*
> *I write to you in haste and a longer letter will soon follow. I am*

*eager to give you this news: I have met the young lady whom I
am convinced will be my wife. Father, I am in love, but this is
no blind passion. She is an exceptional creature, not only beautiful, but intelligent and accomplished and of excellent family. She
speaks perfect French and more than passable English. You will
have guessed she is Spanish, but with a knowledge of our own
culture that is surprising in one so young (she is not yet
seventeen). Besides Balzac, she has read Dickens and George
Eliot. I intend to introduce her now to the works of Walter
Scott. Are there other Scottish writers I should recommend,
what do you think, sir? Burns and Dunbar may be over-taxing
for the words being Scots and perhaps Stevenson is not altogether
suitable.*

*Her musical talents are rare. She has a quite entrancing voice
and is a truly gifted pianist. She plays Liszt and Chopin with
the fingers of an angel and sings the loveliest of French and
German songs. Yet with all this, she is modest and has no
grand opinion of herself. Her name is María del Pilar. My
courtship has scarcely begun, but I am convinced that I will win
her despite the opposition from her family. Will you give me
your blessing, sir?*

*Father, I trust you are well. And Aunt Annabel? I beg you
to assure her of my affectionate regards, and please be so good as
to tell Nettie I was asking after her.*

Your most devoted and respectful son,
Alexander

Joseph had always been Alexander to his father, at least ever
since his mother's death, for Joseph had been her choice of
name, her own father's name, and Hector Finlay had not liked

it, only giving in for his wife's dear sake. At home, both his aunt and the housekeeper had called him Sandy. But Joseph has stayed Joseph to himself.

This first letter is designed, even if obscurely so, to provoke, to alarm, to convey an impression of foolish impulsiveness, even to sting his father by neglecting to acknowledge his own likely opposition while referring to the obstacles that might arise in Spain. It was followed swiftly by the promised longer letter which only mentioned the matter obliquely in a post-script and otherwise related events of business and mutual interest to father and son: the problems in constructing the new drainage channels, the General Manager's handling of the latest strike in the open-cast workings, the new arrivals up at Bella Vista – a family from Bristol – and how this affected the rival camps of English and Scots at the club. Here Joseph is his father's son, sober and surefooted. He awaited a response.

> *My dear Alexander,*
> *I have your two letters and it is my fervent hope that you have come to your senses by now. You must know that I could never countenance a marriage between yourself and a Spanish woman. The letter in which you bring up this matter is disturbingly silent on the details of the girl's family and upbringing, but in any case such a union, with the first and overwhelming obstacle of religion, would be an abomination. If you have proceeded any further in your 'courtship' of this young woman, I entreat you, be steadfast and give her up. Put my mind at rest without delay. I am most troubled and upset.*
>
> > *Your devoted father,*
> > *Hector Forsyth Finlay*

A sheet of flimsy paper escaped from the letter's thick vellum folds. It bore a text:

> A wise son maketh a glad father: but a foolish son is the heaviness of his mother.
>
> (Proverbs 10:1)

This was a quirk of his father's. The Scriptures trawled for *bons mots* of guidance, the Good Book ever apposite.

Joseph's next letter was altogether different, and begged his father's forgiveness most humbly. Of course he understood his father's worries; he saw what a blow his blunt enthusiasm must have delivered and how cruelly selfish he had been. But it was not in his mind to marry against his father's wishes. The matter was not as his father must have imagined.

> . . . *Pilar (her name is María del Pilar de Breda y Gutiérrez Blanco) is no mere ordinary* señorita, *but the granddaughter of a marquess. Her grandmother, who belongs to one of the most illustrious families of the district — indeed, an ancestor sailed with Columbus — possesses three hundred acres of grain fields and vineyards as well as olive groves and several orchards and livestock. It is a small estate by comparison with many in Andalusia, but it yields well, from both produce and tenants, for it is excellently managed; the grain can be relied upon for a good income, for there is a government-set floor on the selling price, and besides exporting wheat the family has sherry interests. Pilar too has substantial inherited wealth from her father, whose only child she was . . .*

★

Joseph's letter, which he saw as a masterpiece of tact and judgement, went on to narrate the tragedy of the shipwreck, omitting however any further reference to Pilar's father, lest his Cuban nationality seem an excess of the foreign.

Pilar's father, Joseph had learned from Andrés, had arrived from Cuba a year or so after Doña Cristina's husband had died. The story went that this scion of impoverished Spanish emigré gentry had befriended the young widow through some distant family connection and made himself useful by helping her deal with the mess of debts and mortgages incurred by her corrupt estate manager. A new manager was taken on, Doña Cristina learned a thing or two herself, Los Robles prospered, and, since Pilar's future father had by now set himself up in business in Huelva and had no wife, it was thought that the pair might marry. Instead, it was to young Cristina, the elder of the widow's two daughters and some twenty years his junior, that the Cuban eventually addressed his suit. Yet how could the mother refuse such a valued friend, one to whom she plainly owed so much?

It was Joseph's belief that this family episode, in which an outsider brought aid and good luck, had a bearing on how he himself had fared in his suit to Doña Cristina for her granddaughter's hand in marriage. For, to begin with, everything seemed against him, a fact that had only spurred him on.

Doña Cristina Gutiérrez Blanco, the daughter of a marquis, though not herself a marquess, despite Joseph's tactical assertion of Pilar's lineage, figured publically among the landowners of the province who had set themselves in opposition to the Company. They deplored its increasing control of the district around the mines, which bypassed the *ayuntamientos* and reduced their own powers; they decried with strident patriotism the foreign ownership of so much Spanish land and assets; they abhorred the Protestant teachers in the Company school; and most vociferously of all, they clamoured against the *teleras*, the practice of burning ores in the open air as a means of calcination.

Each time this was done, and it was almost daily, some three hundred tons of sulphur erupted into the atmosphere as sulphur dioxide.

When there was no breeze the yellow clouds hung thick as a London pea-souper and on one occasion were to blame for a head-on collision between two trains, with resulting catastrophe and loss of life. This tragedy was ghastly to imagine. Windows must have been tight shut before the crash. The glass would have shattered, and as the dying lay amid its shards the toxic haze that covered them must have seemed the very fumes of hell.

If the wind blew in their direction whole villages were forced to retreat inside, taking with them any cats, dogs, livestock and children, and anything that grew, while sealing doors and windows. Geraniums left outside in their pots would wither, and overlooked songbirds would be silenced forever in their cages. For those without a solid shelter and with the lungs of the tubercular it was an ill wind indeed.

In the winter months the prevailing wind tended to blow smoke westwards from the workings to Zalamea la Real, where the best agricultural land lay. Here, and elsewhere, landowners were paid for loss of crops and damaged soil. But this failed to repair blighted pride or ease their sense of being robbed. The scarred landscape was doubly dispiriting as a reminder of the foreign hand that held sway over it. In response, the Anti-Smoke League was born, uniting the landed powers of the province in a bid to impose a ban on this outrage.

It is an ill wind indeed that blows no good, for it was the *teleras* that Joseph used to win his cause. He had met Pilar twice, and his subsequent attempts to call on her had got no further than the maid who answered the front door. Then he wrote to Doña Cristina, a long much-drafted letter declaring his love and giving a persuasive account of himself, his family and his standing. He presented himself as a Company man whose soul was his own, a respecter of others' rights and freedoms, a believer in religious tolerance, sharing none of the bigoted notions and petty-mindedness that were rampant within the stiff-necked precincts of Bella Vista. He also pledged his support in the 'noble and worthy fight' to ban the *teleras*. With his letter, and as evidence that he was not alone in this disaffection, he enclosed a poem penned by a colleague, one John Allan, whose overstretched loyalty and disillusionment had driven him close to resignation. There were some half dozen stanzas in this vein:

> The earth is red, the sky bright blue,
> No tree or green thing breaks the view;
> On every side death reigns supreme,
> For six long miles no life is seen,
> But barren ground and charrèd stumps.

Joseph made sure to apologise for Allan's literary defects; 'I merely wish you to see how heartfelt are the sentiments of loathing for this modern inferno.'

Joseph was invited to visit Los Robles for lunch the following Sunday.

When he stepped inside the house his first impression was of colour and well-engineered shade: the vestibule walls were half-tiled in a patterned white and azure, the floor was inlaid marble and chandeliers of delicate black ironwork hung from the ceiling. At the end of a long broad corridor off which led several passageways he saw an arched opening brilliant with bougainvillaea, and heard the murmur of water tripping on to stone. When he was ushered into the assembled company he realised that Doña Cristina was more shrewd than he had reckoned and did not intend to make things easy for him. The rural dean was there too, and Don José Lorenzo Serrano, the League's most prominent and vocal leader. But Joseph relished his welcome in the ranks of the enemy. He regaled them with stories at the Company's expense: the rivalries between the wives at Bella Vista, the recent stoppages over piecework rates and pay lost on the bad smoke days. He told them of the clerk dismissed for drunkenness and the unannounced departure of one undermanager whose nerves were torn to shreds by 'the heat, the dust, the *teleras* and the damned Bakuninites'.

> *My dear father,*
> *I cannot tell you how happy I am that the family permits me to visit Pilar every Sunday; always chaperoned of course.*
> *I have her reading* The Heart of Midlothian *now. And with a tattered copy of Mr Graham's* Lyric Gems *lent to me by*

Peabody's wife I have taught her one or two Scottish airs. She plays and sings 'Think on Me' with such poignant and tender feeling that it would move you to tears were you to hear her . . .

As Joseph impressed his mother's cornelian ring into the warm softened wax, he pictured his father, in his sombre gaslit study at home or in his office at the Clyde Trustees, with a pewter Glasgow sky outside, reading this, pensive, perhaps even moist-eyed at the thought of the sweet and plaintive air of which his wife had been so fond.

The Bakuninites

The father of Spanish anarchism, if fathers truly have a place in such a passionately anti-authoritarian creed, would have to be the Neapolitan Giuseppe Fanelli, who arrived in Spain in October 1868, shortly after Queen Isabella's flight into exile, as an emissary carrying the message of Bakunin: 'To organise society in such a fashion that every individual, man or woman, coming into life, shall find as nearly as possible equal means for the development of his or her different faculties and for their utilisation by his or her labour; to organise a society which, rendering for every individual, whoever he may be, the exploitation of anybody else impossible, permits each to participate in social wealth.'

Not knowing Spanish, Fanelli spoke in Italian, but his eloquence was not lost on the young Madrid printers, for all that none of them had much understanding of his language and only one possessed a little French with which to bridge so many gaps. The spirit of anarchism found expression nonetheless in Fanelli's hands and eyes and the alternating sad and angry music of his voice, and his listeners were inspired as if by long-awaited revelation. So it was, elsewhere in Spain, wherever he spoke, conveying a vision of hierarchies laid waste by innocent loves and innocent hatreds devoid of concupiscence. Passion allowed to be free from sin.

Why did anarchism flourish in Spanish soil, as it did in France and Italy? One answer is that Catholicism's strict embrace incites to its own furious negation. Its elevation of dogma and its denial of the individual conscience, its absolutism of thought and sanctification of power, in anarchism seem to ignite a rage of desire for their opposite.

Why does the same grape that makes the humble Riesling of the Rhineland transmute into aromatic finos, amontillados and olorosos when planted in the red-brown soil of Jerez and Sanlúcar, hotbeds of anarchism by the by, and likewise in the vineyards of Huelva? That fanaticism which takes plaster saints for target practice before it burns the church down was seen as a mark of those sherry anarchists, who were the bane of both the English and the Spanish magnates of the blonde and copper-coloured drink, and suffered for it cruelly. In the Black Hand trials of '83, seven were garotted in Jerez, thousands jailed. The British Consul argued for the executions.

Copper too had its Bakuninites, some of them first schooled as labourers in the sherry vineyards.

★

From the train window, Pilar, by Joseph's side, gazes out at the river. Purplish red, it resembles an artery, churning with thick blood. Beyond it rise dark cindery hillocks of slag.

When they get out at Río Tinto station the air is choked with pink dust, on the drift of a hot little wind. Pilar knots a chiffon scarf around her hat, unfolds a large white handkerchief and holds it to her mouth.

'You wanted to come, my dear,' says Joseph at once, as if her gestures already vindicate all his opposition.

She nods emphatically.

Joseph is a little angry with himself for having given in to her persistence. He cannot endure her to be peeved with him and she has outdone him in obduracy, threatening never to relinquish this desire, which would plague him forever. Now, as they walk towards the biggest of the workings, he feels a surge of irritation. He feels what he had not quite anticipated: the absurd figure he must cut, walking about here with his Spanish wife on his arm. Ravishing as she is with her fashionably cut suit and her dainty kid boots, she is entirely out of place and bound to make everyone feel ill at ease.

Pilar stands at the top of the rise where the path ends and looks down. It is a strange sight, this first view of something she has heard talked of for years.

There is a deep wide bowl scooped out of the landscape and the pink earth has been dug in tiers and terraces which grow wider towards the bottom. Laid upon them are tracks along which the ore carts trundle, and in the distance she can see several of these moving down towards the calcination ground. Several hundred men are at work down in that dust cauldron, extracting and loading ore, digging out galleries and trenches, raising ladders on which they perch with no apparent care for safety. They are faraway tiny figures and she needs Joseph's commentary to see all this, even with the binoculars. Shouts, hammering, the uneven percussion of pickaxe on rock, the screech of wheels and rails and the clatter of machinery rise in a grating acoustic that rumbles with the intermittent thunder of explosions. Sulphur itches at the nostrils from the *teleras* of the day before. None will burn today; Joseph has confirmed this was so in advance.

Through the binoculars Pilar now notices that a few women toil among the mass of men. It is hard to see their faces, but they wear long skirts and narrow leather aprons.

She can see a vantage point that would take them closer. Joseph says no, but she laughs and pulls him by the arm, trying to drag him back to the path so that they can find the lower route. He resists, catching hold of her hand.

'I said no, Pilar. Pay heed to me. It is no place for you!'

But she frowns and even starts back from his loud angry face, so he tucks her arm in his and softens.

'Listen then, we'll go just a little way down.'

On a lower rim of the huge crater the scale of things below them alters. Now, Pilar can see that the women are young for the most part, some a little younger than herself; a few are perhaps around thirty or more, with haggard eyes and cheeks.

All these faces are dark from the sun, although men and women alike wear broad-brimmed hats tied under the chin. It is just after nine, not hot yet. All the same Pilar feels the unkind grip of her stays get tighter and her kid boots pinch from their newness.

There are not many women, perhaps two score among hundreds, but the sight of her own sex holds her transfixed. When she looks more closely at the men she is struck by how the shape of their hats and their leather overtrousers, split and tied above the knee, give them the look of the American cowboys she has seen in the picture papers; or the figure impressed in relief upon the honey-coloured blocks of saddle soap Roque keeps in the stables. As the soap smoothes and shrinks, el Vaquero rubs away to nothing.

The train has been stalled further down the line with engine trouble. Pilar sits, patient and composed, in a waiting room at the Company offices, relieved to be out of the sun. Matheson's portrait bears down on her. Joseph has left her alone and gone in search of a solution to the problem of her return, his agitation apparent.

Duncan Lister comes to his rescue, for he is leaving to deliver urgent documents to the *ayuntamiento* at Valverde and would be delighted to convey Mrs Finlay back to Los Robles, which is not much out of his way. It would be a long and bumpy ride without any shelter in the dog cart, but it appears to be all that there is. Perhaps he can find Mrs Finlay a more comfortable conveyance should they chance upon any acquaintances going that way.

Pilar finds Duncan Lister amiable. He is a little younger than Joseph and one of the few unmarried men now on the Company staff. He is talkative, his Spanish fluent, but she asks to speak English so that she might have the practice. They leave at a trot.

'We'll slow down, Mrs Finlay, if you're finding it too

bumpy. It's just that I'm in a wee hurry and it's getting hot, you'll have noticed.'

Pilar smiles and opens her tassled parasol, holding it in such a way that it shields Lister too from the sun's blank glare.

They drive down the hill to Río Tinto and out of the town past the first of the mining encampments on its outskirts. Pilar asks Lister if he knows when the Company's house-building programme will be completed. When will there be homes for all the miners' families?

'All? All, Mrs Finlay? Well, that would be asking a lot. But the Company has built a fair number of houses already.'

There were Far West cowboys down in the workings, and now she seems to see the wigwams of Red Indians. Among low huts made of mud and rushes, others nailed together with old timbers and sacking, tall conical tents sprout all over this ragged dustblown settlement. Everywhere there are children, and a great many skinny dogs, as well as occasional pigs that snuffle among the rubbish. Pilar takes cover behind her handkerchief again.

Lister keeps up the jolting pace until the landscape alters, the air smells cleaner and oaks and poplars shade them on the road. Pilar learns that he has been five years with the Company, and is from Edinburgh, where he has a fiancée. She imagines his bride-to-be as hemmed in by chimneys, austere-eyed and clad in high-necked tartan. Ill though this gloomy primness matches Lister's own good nature, Pilar cannot otherwise picture the type of the Company lady.

On Queen Victoria's birthday she had gone, a new bride, to be a guest of the Company on the one day when Spanish wives were welcome at the club. Joseph had drawn her into the circle of ladies. They had given her wan smiles and shaken her hand with a cold, indifferent vigour, asking her nothing beyond the usual courtesies and springing into life only with the start of the day's sports and games. She had watched some stout ladies of forty or so run the egg-and-spoon race, been prevailed upon to wave a paper Union Jack, and met the Acting General Manager, Mr Osborne, who, like several of the men, was attired in white jodhpurs and pith helmet. With tenacious concentration she had listened to the speeches which spoke of Christian duty and hailed the Christian march towards the rout of lawlessness and vice among the natives. She had eaten cucumber sandwiches and, *force majeure* alone compelling her, sipped lukewarm cups of milky tea. With an even greater sense of ceremony and purpose, a toast had been drunk to the Queen. 'Long live her majesty.' Words ringing out with the jubilation of their echo round the globe and back again.

How do you conquer lawlessness? By demonstrating virtue of course, that is pointing out the straight and narrow, though sometimes it is only the finger itself that gets seen in such a gesture. Matheson's experience is dauntless and robust in this respect. He has preached on missions to the whores and down-and-outs of East London. He has travelled from Hampstead to Stepney with messages of everlasting pain and punishment, instilling nausea in the hearts of errant men and women who could only entertain the prospect of repentance with what must have been a trembling luxuriance.

Imagine Bella Vista high atop its hill as a haven of all that is Christianly clean, of crisply laundered percale blouses and white cricket flannels, their creases pressed by native house-maids, of highly polished trophies in the clubroom; while down where that copper-dirty river flows, and all around it, are rank pits of sin: drunkenness, gambling, prostitution, stab-bings, theft and Godlessness. Can those at risk of damnation be saved by philanthropy? Believing so, the Company com-bines it with the legitimate arithmetic of profit and loss, tax relief and compulsory wage deduction. In the mining towns and villages there are Company stores and workmen's clubs where the dynamite blasters and furnace men who drink their *aguardiente* in the mornings, buy Company wine at nights – but not too much of it, for watchful eyes keep Company rules in mind. 'The regulation of liquor' is one of Matheson's fiercest precepts. Likewise the benefits of philanthropy are reg-ulated, rationed and spread thin.

Pilar is quieter than usual that evening, overtired by the jour-ney thinks Joseph, observing her at dinner. As they get ready for bed, Pilar unpinning her hair, Joseph unfastening his col-lar, she tells him she believes she is expecting a child. He tastes an utter bliss of relief.

Tornet

Maximiliano Tornet was dismissed from the Company's employ on August 26, when the Acting General Manager, John Osborne, found him on the south lode open-cast peddling revolutionary newspapers. At Osborne's behest, Tornet was then arrested for selling illegal publications and taken by the Civil Guard to

Valverde del Camino, location of the district's jail and courthouse. A thorough search of his lodgings uncovered revolutionary contacts in Cuba and a notebook stuffed with names of great interest to the Company, so that the following day a dozen or so leaders of anarchist cells were also dismissed from their jobs and reported to the police. Although disturbed by these discoveries, Osborne made capital from the coup. He said the rooting out of trouble and its makers had headed his agenda, and everyone knew him for a man who tackled problems at close quarters. Tornet was his own personal catch.

Tornet had arrived back in Spain four years earlier, having been deported from Cuba for his political activities. The Company had no inkling of this background when they took him on at the mines, even though Tornet's status as a deportee with a political past obliged him to report monthly to the police. Since he was literate and could keep account of figures, he was employed accordingly, first as a weigher, then as a checker. At the time of his arrest he held the job of timekeeper at a new blast furnace. All the while he was agitating and recruiting men to the anarchist cause and building the secret honeycomb of cells within the mines still wider. Four years is a long time to stay undetected, amid intense trade unionism and constant demands from the workforce. Frequent small-scale strikes flared at one or other site: in the open-cast workings or underground, at the blast furnaces or the railway yards. These separate and uncoordinated actions were often tactical, spreading the loss of pay and the burden of organisation, while ensuring disruption to output. For four years Tornet had avoided suspicion and no one betrayed him.

If Osborne, triumphant, felt he had dealt with the source of the Company's troubles at one tidy stroke, then his triumph was short-lived. After being held in prison for two months at Valverde, where he busied himself writing and managed to smuggle out articles for *el Productor* in Havana, so that Cuban tobacco workers might derive some profit from anti-colonial struggle in the colonising power, Tornet was acquitted. The charge had been empty, the incriminating newspapers turned out to have been legally printed under licence. Tornet would have known this and insisted upon it in his imme- diate defence on arrest. Clearly, no one took any notice, such was the fury to have him locked up.

Once he was free, Tornet resumed his political work openly, entering the mines in defiance of the Company, selling tracts and newspapers and addressing meetings. Without wages, he had no income, but anarchist work- ers collected funds in compensation. Agitating out in the open, moving about untramelled by working duties or discipline, he represented even more of a threat than before. Osborne issued orders to the head of the Company guard that if seen on any workings Tornet was not to be ejected but arrested and held prisoner for the day. He informed the mayor of this decision.

Tornet was not to be deterred. The Company guards succeeded in catching him from time to time, but with the miners' protection he usually eluded them, being well hidden by the time they arrived or having fled to another part of the mines. He even formed alliances with the Communists, rivals in recruitment.

Osborne then went a step further and wrote to the Civil Governor requesting that the bothersome and dangerous agitator be forcibly removed to another district well away from the mines. The Civil Governor refused.

She calls it her sewing room, and in it she has trays laid out with embroidery silks in different finenesses and colours, and she has done some work recently on the yoke of a nightgown and on a cradle counterpane, though she lacks the flair and skill for truly delicate stitching. She is no born needlewoman; lately she is clumsy with the heat and her tiredness and a new impatience that has come as her body has grown heavier and her ankles swell. She pricks her fingers and the tiny globe of blood sinking into the linen distresses her; she finds cuts and bruises on her hands and cannot think how they got there.

So she has put away her sewing.

It is cooler here than anywhere else in the house, but she still feels languid, the fan shivering in her hand as she lies on a *chaise longue* in the somnolent afternoon in a muslin wrap, propped up with cushions, while the *abuela* rests, receiving no visitors, and the servants have retreated from the corridor bustle of the morning and lunch. This languor makes her feel vacant and ungainly, in the wrong element, like some amphibious creature that has stayed too long on land. She broods.

Books have become the best distraction, albeit a guilty one, for reading neglects the baby inside her, the one who should fill her mind and occupy her hands with tasks in preparation for his coming. Instead she wants to seize on other things before it is too late, before she is carried away into being that new person: mother. She feels no discontent, only curiosity, and no one is stopping that, for Joseph wants her mind to grow, he tells her so, showing her books: Rousseau, Hobbes, Adam Smith, German philosophers and poets; reading to her: from Tennyson and from Smollet's *Humphry Clinker*, both favourites of his, and always the novels of Walter Scott for which he had a boyhood love. Her curiosity. About what? Or is it that she only wants to *have* again that faculty, which she has lost somewhere in all that has befallen her. The breathlessness of courtship, a time of delight and trepidation, when Joseph's presence alone made her tremble and break into smiles, when she spent whole days pleading with her grandmother for him to be listened to; persuading, succeeding through tears and argument. And then to be stunned by married sexual pleasure, sent into a daze of the senses that shocked. And now more strange happenings in the body . . .

Alteration seemed to flow around her, draw her on in its own quick stream, and has left her now high and dry, though with everything she wanted. So she reads to discover what she might want to know.

Whatever she seeks, she seeks it elsewhere now than in Joseph's cherished volumes. Except for his Bible, which for her, as a Catholic, is a matter of transgression, although venial. The Bible and Las Casas, which she has often read before, for her ancestor Juan de Castro travelled with him to the Indies and stood among his followers when he went to petition the king in Seville – what tragic threads of history join these inland shores to the Americas.

Las Casas' outrage at the fate of the Indians fills her with pride and with shame. An extravaganza of torture, death and maiming, of bodies burned and ripped open, whipped and branded, impaled, amputated and blinded; a multiplication of all the martyrdoms Christendom has known. Las Casas' litany of torment and injustice was inspired, she knows, by Scripture, by the Word.

She has Joseph's Bible in her lap. He reads it only and always when letters arrive from his father. These come with a text in their folds or a chapter and verse for Joseph to look up. He lifts the book down from the shelf and thumbs the silk-thin pages to show her:

> The eternal God is thy refuge, and underneath are the everlasting arms
>
> (Deuteronomy 33:27)
>
> A father of the fatherless, and a judge of the widows, is God in His holy habitation
>
> (Psalms 68:5)

This one, she was sure, was meant for herself and the *abuela*.

> The fathers have eaten sour grapes, and the children's teeth are set on edge
>
> (Ezekiel 18:2)
>
> In all labour there is profit, but the talk of the lips tendeth only to penury
>
> (Proverbs 14:23)
>
> Wine maketh merry, but money answereth all things
>
> (Ecclesiastes 10:19)

Shall mortal man be more just than God? Shall a man be
more pure than his maker?

(Job 4:17)

He that contemneth small things shall fall little by little
(Ecclesiasticus 19:1)

These texts with their blindly omniscient commentary disturb and sometimes anger her, however sardonic Joseph's
response. Is the text but an unerring weapon that will always
find its mark, however ill-directed? Is God not being mocked
by such presumption on the Word?

Reading for herself, she finds that the Bible is indeed a
book for all seasons, and sees how easy it would be to contradict the bald warnings and counsels of her father-in-law. Yet
how impossible to imagine such a thing. Only look at Hector
Finlay's photographic likeness in its fine silver frame, hugely
bearded and whiskered, made monumental by his saturating
bulk. He is wealthy, righteous, and unassailable by any woman.
Beside him on the wall of their bedroom, Joseph's mother in
oils, a small painting that shows her young, pale-haired and
half-smiling, her shoulders fading, almost wing-like, in the
muddy subfusc of the background, which accentuates a child-
like, ethereal face.

The stifling afternoons of late summer give way to autumn,
the stillness replaced by sounds that carry in the thinner air:
the sporadic gunshot of hunters, the barking of their dogs.
Pilar scarcely leaves this well-ordered house whose rhythms
and rituals adjust themselves continually to her need for sleep,
for peace in the courtyard or garden or orchard, for delicacies

and all manner of sweets. She is a queen and the house holds its breath in anticipation of a prince's birth.

On Christmas Eve Joseph asks her to sing at the piano, but she says she is weary of her music. She weeps. In the festive days that follow he often finds her praying, too often for his liking or his understanding.

Gently he takes her in his arms, he rubs her feet and ankles with jasmine and lavender oils, he whispers soft words and when she cries he wipes away her tears.

In their aftermath, the events of early February appeared confused, whitewash on the one hand, fear on the other creating a cloud of obscurity that hangs over them to this day. Subsequent official accounts contained glaring gaps and inconsistencies too numerous to be overlooked, not even attempting to justify some of the most shocking aspects of what happened, yet disclaiming the Company's responsibility, using adjectives like 'unfortunate' and 'regrettable', with that bureaucratic gloss where English understatement clothes hypocrisy. Matheson, who arrived belatedly from London, saw it as a bad case of mismanagement, in which there had been insufficient recognition that the natives, undisciplined and backward as they were, had to be treated accordingly. They were no more than children. In this, he compared them with the Irish.

For years, the Company had battled with discipline, imposing escalating fines on those late for the start of a shift. But punctuality persisted as a problem. So did the eight-hour day demand and opposition to the work gang system, where up to twelve men shared out pay between them on a piecework rate calculated in advance; if one man tired and lagged behind everyone would suffer. On those rare occasions when protest strikes won changes to a day-wage system, output fell immediately. Then, the stark correlation between productivity and payment would be restored at the earliest opportunity, whatever the agreement.

The situation had gradually worsened. Not only did managers have a hostile workforce to contend with, but the *teleras* had made them other, powerful enemies. A moment came when all these forces coalesced against the Company in an alliance as formidable as it was surprising.

On the evening of February 2, William Rich, the new General Manager, who had only recently arrived in Spain for the first time, informed the British staff that they should stay indoors with their families and keep shotguns and revolvers at the ready. Most of the men possessed twelve-bores for Sunday shooting and certain dressing-table drawers might contain a dainty, pearl-handled lady's revolver untouched and wrapped in velvet. Those who had no arms were to be supplied with revolvers and ammunition from the Company arsenal. The compound mentality was already well ingrained. Now a double guard had been posted at Bella Vista.

Rich had little foreknowledge of what trouble was in store for him when he set out from London and he masks a slight panic by assuming a posture of stiff, calm authority. He is a man of only medium height, but the neat white beard and well-tailored sack suit lend him a new-minted businesslike presence. He was hasty in dismissing Osborne's advice, he knows now, but intends to repair this error by rallying the senior staff around him.

It is late when Joseph reaches Los Robles. Pilar hears the

commotion of horses' hooves and from the window watches as the lanterns bob towards her, fidgeting with the fringes of her shawl, pulling it more closely round her shoulders as Joseph's face looms nearer, smothered in the light.

He is tired and distracted, he touches the mound of her belly, inquires how she is, but fails to meet her eyes.

The god of productivity is a demanding deity, never satisfied. Giving your all is not enough. Giving more is a trap that will prove you are dispensable – perhaps not you, but your uncle or your sister's husband, or the man next to you who walked from Badajoz last year to find a job to feed his starving children. How many of you walked here a year or a decade ago? More than came in carts, I'm sure of it. You came on foot from Jaén and Baeza, from as far as León and Orense, from the Pyrenees foothills and across the frontier in Portugal. And did the Company ever pay you for those blisters? Now, for a few *reales* more they want your bodies wrecked and exhausted. They want you to work even harder so that all you have left at the end of each day is the husk of a man and perhaps less than that, for you'll have torn muscles and worse, broken bones and lungs filled with dust. And the god of productivity will have no use for you. And all the sooner if the men who are now paid less can work just as hard.

Thus Tornet addressed the railway wagon loaders, who had been offered a bonus to up tonnage in line with temporary hands being taken on at lower rates. Accumulated stocks of ore had to be loaded for export. They lay untouched. The loaders refused to see an undercutting of their rates and the strike began on the first of February.

In that same final week of January, at the calcining ground the loaders were told that they could fill four wagons in the time it had taken to fill three; new machinery could now speed up their work. Because of this the rate per wagon would be cut.

'Mechanisation is the capitalist's way of turning men into machines.'

The loaders needed little persuasion; the machine is a natural enemy whose only rationale is to serve productivity and profits for the capitalist, and is liable moreover to slice off a finger or a foot.

What provoked most of all in this week of provocations occurred at the San Dionisio workings. Softer rock is making excavation easier. The coming month's contracts will lower rates to take account of this. But they make no provision for the rock getting harder again. The result: wages halved unless the miners double the quantity of ore they extract.

'Everything they do, not just to you but for you, is to bring wages down.'

Whatever the level of pay, which is never kept constant but is forever vulnerable to adjustment too complicated to be trusted, each employee forfeits one peseta weekly towards the medical facilities of which the Company is so proud. The ending of this levy is another of the strikers' demands.

For the first time the entire workforce is urged to strike in solidarity. Thousands answer the unprecedented call. On the morning of February 1, only thirty men report for work, protected by a contingent of the *guardia civil* and the Company's armed guard.

★

Tornet the strategist; no wild-eyed fanatic, but sharp in mind and instinct. That the Bakuninite and the wealthy *cacique* should have formed an alliance observes one cardinal rule of anti-colonial struggle, of which the former had experience in plenty: first join forces with the enemy at home to defeat the foreign one you have in common. But did he have illusions when he shook the hand of Serrano and his son-in-law Ordóñez, and drank their *fino* at a meeting of the League in some smart Huelva drawing-room, where the glasses are Bohemian crystal and cigars sit in chased silver boxes. Serrano, tall, lean and eagle-faced; a boss, a fixer, a millionaire in the making, relishing power with a lusty enjoyment that gives his features a permanent thin smile. The smile of the born winner, whose certainty humbles more than any scowl can, for it takes compliance for granted. Ordóñez, the right-hand man whose role it is to contain and absorb what his father-in-law is not; handsome, big-framed, with a quiet, almost deliberately restrained manner that some find faintly threatening. Although no fool, Ordóñez lacks Serrano's sureness. He is a man who will count on wealth coming to him rather than on any talent for creating it. He is the subordinate who anticipates problems and smoothes them into challenges for one who takes deep pleasure in being a well-advantaged adversary, whatever the game. In the Anti-Smoke League, Serrano has nothing to lose. If victory does not ensue from his leadership and machinations, the outrage he exploits will only grow.

Had Tornet done this kind of thing in Havana? Perhaps he turned down that *fino*, either out of pride or asceticism.

The planning of it was leisurely, done deep in anti-macassered armchairs and plush-upholstered sofas. But when the day came no time was wasted. At the first stop in Calañas the mayor received them with coffee and obsequious assurances of action. Serrano was indeed feared and behind him stood a powerful clique. Tornet was notorious. An order immediately went out instructing the Tharsis mines to end the *teleras* by February 20.

Zalamea bore the brunt of the smoke. There the mayor had his own principles, and, as it happened, a heart, besides depending on Serrano for the votes that got him elected. When the latter strode in with Tornet and Ordóñez, he had therefore not a moment's hesitation. But it did surprise him to see Serrano treat Tornet almost like a son, courting him, bent on conquering the younger man's aloofness, while the son-in-law was more taciturn than usual.

They paid these visits, and others to town halls in the area, on horseback. Tornet's chestnut mare was doubtless loaned to him, well lathered and brushed each evening in Serrano's stables.

By February 1, all the town halls had issued orders to ban the *teleras*. All except Nerva, and Río Tinto, which belonged after all to the Company, every last stick and stone of it.

On the first day of the strike the Civil Governor in Huelva had sent reinforcements to the ten-strong *guardia civil* at the mines. These thirty-five men were, puzzlingly it seemed to Rich, withdrawn as soon as the Río Tinto Civil Guard lieutenant sent a telegram to Huelva advising that things were under control. It was the departure of the short-lived reinforcements that prompted Rich to call his staff together and give them the warning to arm.

Joseph could see that Rich was floundering. He also knew that he himself was seen as a go-between of sorts and that something was expected of him, but something subtle that would let Rich save face, keep his brittle authority intact. Rich had ignored Osborne's advice on cutting tonnage rates more gradually at San Dionisio and was obviously regretting it.

Joseph knew Serrano. Risking nothing, he had spoken out at the club against the *teleras* and it was no secret that he had attended two meetings of the Anti-Smoke League. He racked his brains to find how this could make a difference. Things had gone too far by now. Subtle was beside the point.

Rich let his composure collapse when the meeting dispersed and Joseph was alone with him. What could he offer but his support? Rich asked him to stand by. They shook hands on it. Rich was trembling.

The following afternoon fourteen telegrams flew between Río Tinto and the Huelva authorities, with the Civil Guard commander begging for help in the end. The morning had been quiet but at the stroke of midday something disturbing occurred, disturbing because obviously pre-arranged and yet not at all calm. To Joseph Finlay, who witnessed it in the company of Rich and the Civil Guard commander on their way to the mines from Río Tinto town hall, it assumed the quality of a ritual, a deliberate frenzy. It was with relief that they reached the Company office when they did.

On the stroke of midday thousands emerged from doorways and alleys, clogging the streets and the town hall square. People at once clustered around the men who jumped up on makeshift platforms – crates or wobbly chairs – to address all those in earshot. These speeches by the anarchist and communist cell leaders vied in passion and in recklessness; they called for fairer wages at first, an end to piecework, for the eight-hour day, the abolition of the levy, for full pay on bad smoke days, for better housing. But, as the crowds responded cheering, they added other grievances, words sparked from group to group and inflamed a bolder rhetoric. Among the fevered voices three demands rang loudest. Chase the foreign capitalists from Spain. Land to the landless. Justice for all.

The Civil Guard commander watched helpless from a distance. With just nine men at his disposal he could make no arrests for this inflammatory talk.

At twelve-thirty the mayor and town councillors sent a telegram to Huelva resigning in disgust at the Governor's failure to come to their rescue. By three o'clock there were eight thousand in the streets. At four a shout went up that blacklegs were at work in the south lode and an angry human wave flowed off in that direction. Having chased away the blacklegs and the guards protecting them, the crowd attacked site offices and storehouses in a fury of destruction.

In desperation the Civil Guard lieutenant seeks out Rich to urge his intervention. Rich and Joseph turn towards the door, alarmed as he approaches, revolvers at the ready should the visitor prove dangerous. An initially heated exchange takes place during which Rich refuses point blank to confront the crowd, then the three men talk more calmly.

When the lieutenant made his appearance at the top of the town hall steps no one noticed him at first. But he had a deep powerful officer's baritone and by dint of shouting he managed to quieten those at the front of the square. He told them that their proposals would be dealt with if they appointed representatives to meet him. He would convey what they wanted to the Company in the knowledge that everything possible would be done to resolve all their grievances.

An hour later twenty separate delegations came to him, each with a set of demands.

The lieutenant advised Rich not to reject them but to delay his answer for another twenty-four hours.

They set out from Zalamea where the two contingents came together. Certain mythologised accounts put Tornet alone at the head of the procession, alone, that is, with his unlikely allies: Serrano and his son-in-law, Ordóñez. A strange trinity, on horseback, with the dirty onion-breathed rabble at their backs; four thousand strong at least, perhaps five or even more. This is a frozen cinemascope image, epic and complete.

The ride to Río Tinto. A slow ride with so many on foot, some with banners demanding justice and freedom and an end to wage slavery, a few carrying shotguns or sticks. They have come from el Ventoso, Traslasierra, Delgadas, Zalamea, Madroño and elsewhere. There are women with and without children at their skirts or in their arms; there are even dogs. Bands are playing.

But these people feel too passionate to be festive, they want nothing less than the end of the world, of the world as they know it, with its squalor and punishing labour, its tyrannies. They see empires and faiths as there to be wrecked so that a new world might rise from their ruins. Just as nature tolerates its blasting and destruction by drought and wind and ice and hail and fire, yet struggles back to grow again, so the phoenix of freedom will rise for them from revolution's ashes at some fragile future dawn. This day of new reckoning seems to bring it nearer. But exaltation is not the same thing as festivity.

It is cloudy and cold, then there appears in the sky what Joseph Finlay, at the mines, would call a bore of blue. It funnels out a glimmer of bright sunlight. It is so sweetly in keeping that some of the walkers look up and smile with knowing eyes. Somewhere over the rainbow.

It really isn't far, down that hill which nearly all of them have walked before, though not like this. Exaltation is its own victory, the triumph of empowerment, however close the moment of defeat. It is the conditional for a moment made present and emphatically indicative.

Among that procession walks a fifteen-year-old girl who is not a María of this or that attribute or virtue or place as are so many of the women, but whose name is Anarchy, and a boy the same age called Justice, two of several children born in Cadiz province of mothers who chose to ignore the baptismal font and blessed their infants with rash hopes instead of prayers and holy water.

A rabble is something to be feared, and most of all when it truly knows its enemies are not just of the moment, but that they cast the very mould of this world as it is and as it should not be.

The town is swelled already by a multitude that welcomes them with cheers. Up through the narrow climbing streets and into the slope of the square they ride, Tornet at the head now,

Serrano and Ordóñez behind him and abreast. They dismount at the town hall steps and enter the building, together with the mayor of Zalamea and delegates from all the other villages. The Civil Guard lieutenant and his nine-strong troop look on in silence.

Tornet's voice is low but commanding: 'You must sign.' And the mayor of Río Tinto, slumped in a red brocaded chair, pale with a fear that is lulled by the presence of Serrano, whom he knew well in his youth, answers, sighing, 'It would have no validity in the circumstances.'

What does Tornet's demand have to do with what's being shouted in the square outside: 'Less work, more pay, an end to oppression'? Is Tornet a prey to wilfulness, a man whose hatred of authority means he always has to win though wisdom dictates otherwise. What do the *teleras* matter if there is a bigger battle to be won? Tactics? Honour?

The council chamber overlooks the square. It has tall curtained windows with shutters pulled back. You can see the mass of people beyond if you turn and look away from the two groups of antagonists, a score or so of angry men. Serrano is there at the window and now he signals to Ordóñez. They take their leave, to wait for the outcome somewhere nearby: 'It would be more fitting.' Tornet nods in agreement, they hurry downstairs to the rear of the building, where the horses are tethered, and gallop away. No one heeds the haste of their departure, so intent is the business of argument. For now, no one heeds the spectacle beginning in the square.

Telegrams despatched to London, then from London to Madrid – to an embassy and two ministries – and then the wires buzzed with messages to Huelva. Unforeseen pathways of influence that swayed the loyalty Serrano and Ordóñez had counted on.

The Civil Governor of Huelva's change of heart has brought him here in person. At Río Tinto station he was met by the troop of Civil Guard and cavalry who had arrived unnoticed late the night before. With them was the contingent of soldiers from the Tharsis mines whose transfer he himself had requested. Further reinforcements were due soon from Seville.

They forced their way through thickly crowded streets and no one tried to stop them; just a few stones thrown from upstairs windows. The Governor reached the town hall with the crowd's pandemonium of demands almost shattering his ears. In the council chamber more cacophony, this time shunning him. He abandoned his futile efforts to address the gathering and compel Tornet to leave, opened a window and went on to the balcony. Below, two long lines of soldiery now confronted the square.

Stones were hurled at the balcony. Their target commanded the crowd to disperse and threatened them with violence. But his bellowed words might well have been whispers for all that people heard of them.

Someone rapped out, 'Fire!'

Someone. The lieutenant colonel of the Civil Guard was later to deny having given that order. Yet there was a long and fatal lapse of time before he countermanded it.

Doubtless a whole eternity passed between the instant when those at the front of the crowd saw the two lines of uniforms alter their formation: the front row kneeling to shoot low, the second standing to aim above their heads into the mass of vulnerable flesh that packed the rising slope of the square – and the moment when the golden dash of gunshot hit its mark and ripped through skin and guts and bone. An eternity fractured only by screams and the bright gush of blood, and flailing arms and stumbling feet on cobblestones, and the wailing of children and the hoarse tearing sound of grief, and the absence of sound altogether as life stopped for some forever.

In the hectic wake of that unhurried countermanding order came the final drama of accusation, when Tornet stepped on to the balcony and shed a sobbing catalogue of curses upon the troops below. To the crowd he roared with all the prac-ticed power of his orator's lungs: 'The real enemies of our country are not the English capitalists but the Spaniards them-selves.'

'Shoot him!' A half-dozen men angled their sights at the balcony, but he turned and, like Serrano and Ordóñez before him, fled running three steps at a time to the rear of the building, leapt astride the glossy chestnut mare and rode off. An exit whose triteness and excitement amaze in equal measure.

When the guns had cleared the square there remained forty-eight dead, dying and otherwise wounded, and a crim-son-stained litter of what was lost or torn and broken in the crush of flight for survival. Some of the wounded had been dragged or crawled away and blood trails now led into side streets and alleys. Sounds receded into fragments: scattering feet, shutters banging close at hand, howls of panic rushing to the edge of town and further.

A teenage boy, three women and a one-year-old child were among the dead gathered up in the square.

The wounded lying there were taken to the little hospital in Río Tinto, under guard. After treatment, they were to be moved to the prison at Valverde. As for the rest of the wounded, blood trails were followed. Arrests were made in Río Tinto and as cavalry brutal as cossacks swept the roads west to Zalamea, east to Nerva and south to El Madreño. Through the days that followed, the Civil Guard searched house-to-house in all of the villages and encampments. In some they found wounded and dying, for no one dared to seek help from doctors.

The unfound dead were buried secretly among the slag, their cinder-crusted skeletons dug out at intervals across the years. Tornet, most hunted of the fugitives, was sighted by a guard in Zalamea but never was discovered, remaining as elusive as any legend. After a month he was deemed to be in Portugal and the search was given up. The tender-hearted mayor of Zalamea made his escape to Madrid and went into hiding. Many of the men without families sought wilderness refuge in the mountains or returned to their places of origin, walking back to Cáceres or Cádiz or León.

At the windows of the great white house mourning shutters are drawn. Pilar cannot kneel, she is too encumbered and her legs are weak, so she lies on the *chaise longue*, and weeps as she prays:

De profundis. Out of the depths I have cried to thee, oh Lord . . .

Only a single candle flickers in the early evening gloom. Joseph returns home at six and then the lamp beside her will be lit.

Elsewhere, at Bella Vista, trunks are being locked and secured, others waiting for their owners in Cádiz or in Huelva. Resignations began on the Monday after the massacre, several families have sailed by now; better to face the Bay of Biscay in February than go in fear of maddened outlaws hell-bent on revenge. At the mines, where work has since resumed, strict checks are being kept on dynamite stocks and their use overseen. Mistrust keeps guilt in abeyance. On his arrival from London, Matheson looked set to make far-reaching changes. More decisions referred back to him, a cavalry barracks to be built on the hill overlooking the south-lode open cast, a tighter rein on discipline.

Mourning darkens everything. The earth closes over. In the ring of villages surrounding Río Tinto some pray, those without faith in a god can only weep together, while others pray on their behalf.

'The bread of the needy is their life,' writes Pilar, 'he that taketh away his neighbour's living slayeth him, and he that defraudeth the labourer of his hire is a bloodshedder.'
(Ecclesiasticus 34:21–2)

Joseph is gathering up his papers when Matheson detains him and shows him the letter.

Mr Matheson,
I make so bold as to offer you a text from the Book which my

> *husband tells me is your guiding light, in the hope that justice*
> *will begin to teach your heart its ways . . . Bartolomeo de las*
> *Casas was moved by these words to defend those deprived of life*
> *and land in the Indies.*

'Your wife is impertinent.'

'She is near her confinement, sir.'

'Then she is hysterical. You will need to keep a check on
her temperament.'

'Indeed, sir. I am sorry for this. Forgive her.'

Matheson flicks away the words of Hector Finlay's boy with
half-closed eyes and the hint of a nod.

The child is born one early April afternoon when the air is
translucent, rinsed clear of winter as if once and for all. They
are soon to move from Los Robles and have their own household in the lodge, much nearer to the railway halt, now that
the building work has been completed.

Joseph now has a son but as yet feels no tenderness for him.
This baby with his coal black fuzz of hair and coffee-bean eyes
is too shockingly unlike himself. Spanish blood notwithstand-
ing, he had expected something of the Finlays to prevail. But
he knows he must grow fond of the boy and is sure that in
time this will come.

Postscript

Hugh McKay Matheson died in 1898, the year in which Spain
lost its last colony, Cuba. The *teleras* ceased in 1904. The
mines were returned to Spain in 1954, under Franco.

Faits Divers, August 1927

Germaine Jolivet's shooting of her lover is reported in *La Vigie*. During the year he has worked as chauffeur to the English painter Noel Mirlees, Georges Roussel has often been away. Now, after a week without news, and suspecting infidelity, Germaine has followed him here from Paris. They argue in a restaurant, fiercely, and are asked to leave, without having eaten. They walk back to Georges' shabby room in the *bout du quai*, and the row continues, getting angrier, louder. 'Is that any way to treat a woman!' some neighbours shout when they hear Germaine's screams, in no doubt that Georges is beating her. Then three gunshots. Two miss completely, one grazes a forearm. Before long, the police arrive. Her face pressed against the wall, Germaine is weeping. Georges sits on the bed, eyes blank, as if stunned.

At Varengeville, along the coast, André Breton hunts owls in the woods surrounding the Manoir d'Ango. It is here, in a hut artificially camouflaged with shrubbery, that he has begun writing *Nadja*. Nadja is beautiful, passionate, capricious, mad; a woman made for men's dreams.

> . . . *now the tower of the Manoir d'Ango explodes and a snow-fall of feathers from its doves dissolves on contact with the earth of the great courtyard once paved with scraps of tiles and now covered with real blood.*

From prison in Milan, Antonio Gramsci writes to his wife's sister Tatiana describing the death of a sparrow from a stroke.

> *He cried out like a child . . . but died only the following day: his right side was paralysed and he had to drag himself painfully to eat and drink . . . What I liked in this sparrow was his resistance to being handled. He would rebel fiercely, beating his wings and pecking my hand with great energy . . . I think his spirit must have been eminently Goethean ('Uber allen Gipfeln').*

In his cell another sparrow, tamer, servile, has replaced the dead bird. The letter marks nine months of imprisonment.

On the sea-front near the Casino, where Yvette Guilbert is this week's star attraction, the police arrest Anna Haavikko, twenty-three, Finnish, for possession of a knife and a revolver. Before the magistrate, her lawyers plead that the current situation in Finland makes possession of arms a common occurence. A small fine is imposed, along with a suspended sentence. When arrested she was staring out to sea, hatless, her pale hair wispy in the wind. She was fingering the gun, her thoughts elsewhere. It was low tide and gulls had gathered along the sandy shoreline, facing the waves. Perhaps she was homesick, or perhaps, with the reluctant northerner's sense of release, only glad to have left the even more fathomless greyness of the Nordic sky up there in the past. If she were to turn her back, then this was surely where the south began, on this lip of stony beach. Spasmodic drops of rain were falling. The weather this August has made it the most dismal for years.

In Charlestown gaol near Boston, Nicola Sacco and Bartolomeo Vanzetti, anarchists, walk to their execution. Waiting six years for their death to be final, this shoemaker and this fish-peddler have become known to millions, in New York and Moscow, London and Geneva, in every great city of the world. Now, as they walk to the electric chair, they sing. Voices that soar and tremble sing Mario's aria from the last act of *Tosca:* '*E lucevano le stelle* . . .'; their farewell to life, to the brightness of the stars and the fragrance of the earth in the land where they were born. Their places of birth are far apart, almost as far as Italy's north and south can be, separated by diet and dialect in a country where the language of music is the one still most shared. Vanzetti was born in Villafalletto on the narrow Grana river which runs only a little way from its source in the Alps to join the Po. Sacco in Torremaggiore, on the edge of the sun-blasted Puglia plain that then swells out to become the verdant hilly promontory of the Gargano, Italy's bootspur, sending out green sparks over the sea's sheer blueness: the Tremiti islands.

Were it a hotter August in Paris, the whole of the city would ignite. All through the night demonstrators rule the streets.

Shots are fired, windows smashed, scenes of devastation and looting erupt across the boulevards, Hausmann's strategic channels for the containment of chaos. Among the wreckage everywhere, worst on Sébastopol, scattered placards and banners read 'Sacco and Vanzetti shall not die'. What seismic register can measure the world's shock at the unjust deaths of a cobbler and a fish-peddler, its tremors of rage, its spasms of love and anger, all the convulsive fury of a final struggle already overcome. Down on the Seine, what chaos has flung overboard, things bereft of ownership, floating, bobbing: a tennis racket, a lampshade, a wedding dress, a shoal of unmatched shoes. In the place de l'Etoile a group of men pisses on the flame that burns by the tomb of the unknown soldier – dousing it.

From Morval, where the cliff curves out and away from the bay, Louis Aragon sets off down the steep path. To reach Dieppe for the demonstration he will drive from Pourville, or be driven. When he enters the Terasse several women turn and stare. Whether they like it or not, their eyes are on an object of desire: tall, blue-eyed, an impassive object; militant charmer. His friend Breton is too absorbed by his writing to be joining him there as half-promised, so perhaps it is his ever unpunctual lover Nancy who will come. Nancy Cunard, the absconded heiress with the downturned mouth and the wide, stubborn eyes. One of Nancy's passions is for ivory: African bracelets by the double armful, stern deities and intransigent masks. In the run-down bars of the *bout du quai* she and Aragon have gone in search of sailors who will sell her what they've brought from West Africa's ports. Nothing carved here in this town, famous for centuries for its ivory-work, is of interest to her: the finely-wrought portraits, the fans, the exquisite architecture of scaled-down palaces, the hinged cases for tobacco leaves and the tableaux of wretched poverty after Victor Hugo. A labour that strained eyes; a froth of creamy powder with each minute incision. As the craft died, its masters came to violent ends: murder, suicide; an elephant's curse.

In Le Havre, an agent of the Sûreté, having been discovered as an infiltrator in the committee for solidarity with Sacco and Vanzetti, is stabbed. His condition is critical.

A certain Lady Bailey, holder of a world altitude record, makes the first solo flight by a woman across the Irish Sea.

Another shooting. After arriving from England on the ferry, a Birmingham man named Robert Friel hires a taxi to take him to Rouen for the day, and back again. The return journey is nearly over, when, at St Aubin, he asks the driver to stop and fetch him cigarettes from the *tabac* by the crossroads. Friel takes his opportunity, jumps out of the cab, and disappears, his fare unpaid. Heading for the station over the fast-flowing stream of the Scie, and seeing there's no lucky train, he strikes out across the fields for Offranville, easily eluding his pursuer in the dark. Later that night, when the police visit his hotel, he fires on them. No one but Friel is hurt in the ensuing exchange of shots; a flesh-wound on his shoulder. Once in custody, he confesses his readiness to die, says he's a desperate man, in flight from impossible gambling debts.

★

At night among the beech trees, where it is moist underfoot from the rain, Breton wills an encounter with a lovely naked woman. She would be a *tabula rasa* whatever her guise, Circe or Melusine. Trotsky, whose latest work Breton had bought just before first meeting Nadja in the street, wrote: *The creative union of the conscious with the unconscious is what one usually calls 'inspiration'. Revolution is the inspired frenzy of history.* In the centre of the courtyard of the Manoir d'Ango stands a colossal hive, its dark rafters packed with doves.

When there is nothing else, the *gobiers* eat seabirds, trapping the young ones as they loiter, flightless, on the beach. Sometimes a fledgling tumbles from a high nest on a roof up in town, and wanders to and fro beneath it, foolish and ungainly, every so often attempting flight but failing, until it dies of hunger or falls prey to a dog. You can catch them easily, never mind the frantic beating wings, whose span is nearly that of the adult's, only they are greyer. The *gobiers* scavenge more fruitfully from the sea than from the land, whose rejects they are, pushed to its extremity and below. Outside the *gobes*, pitting the cliffbase like mouseholes in a wainscot, tides and seasons tyrannise, and families implore the August squalls to end. Inside there is chill, tubercular dampness, and everything – broken pots and dishes, the pallets and blankets people sleep on, even the shrimp-nets – is smoke-blackened from the cooking fires. They burn when it is cold, and always at night, and from out at sea, far enough for distance to charm and deceive, they glimmer with the lure of ancient, mythic lights.

Rooms Conducive
to Dreams

Sometimes I lie awake in my vast bed and remember my whole life. These times in the night are dark spaces that draw me into my body. As I feel, enlarged, the power of touching in my fingers, the restlessness of my limbs, the me that is bodily and the me that is brain and memory become uncoupled and enter the depth of the past. Then it is as if the memory itself will expand and envelope me. After a while I become dizzy, a little breathless, and I turn on the light.

I wonder what my younger self would have thought of me now. How much of her is in me, how much of me was in her. Am I perhaps a different person altogether, a woman made only through circumstance and opportunity? I suspect most people to whom I'm known in Paris would picture my past as one of struggle. They've got me down for someone who has risen the hard way, from 'humble origins'. Foreigness is always a good disguise for those, which is why they suspect them; it's a kind of capital, too. I don't just mean the asset of another language, but the distance you get on things from being a lit-tle way outside. You have to be in the know to take advantage of that; it's no use being naive or indifferent. Outside *and* inside. Once you're there, you're on your way, and people will believe you know something they don't.

I find it useful that they're not quite convinced by my gen-tility, that air of distinction with which I welcome guests to the hotel. Perhaps they think I don't really own the establish-ment, even though it bears my name, and everyone knows me as Madame Lear.

The truth is that I come from an upper-crust background. At least in my childhood the family was wealthy, and there had always been 'breeding'. As I grew up, some land and property were sold off, but we were never poor, except in the way the very rich mean. There was a house in Buckinghamshire; it stood in wooded grounds, not lost in the country though, but with a village on our doorstep. No one ever lived in the gatekeeper's lodge, and a Russian vine grew round it, neglected and withering at times, but always reviv-ing. I was happy enough as a child, though solitary. At school most of the village children ignored me. I saw both awe and contempt in their eyes, in their smiles. A kind of fear this was, I realise, not of me, but of my class. At home I had no siblings. I had come late on the scene, long after my brothers, who had both gone away when I was in my infancy, one to join the army, the other to study for the priesthood, and then to the 'mission fields', as my parents always called them.

When I was sent to boarding-school, at eight, I felt no ter-rible wrench from my home and my parents. Though I missed them, it was a relief to be among others of my age.

What I missed most was the house. I'd spent contented hours there, in the dereliction of the top floor, silent and smelling of ancient damp. My secret kingdom, where no one else came, where I scorned time and could sit for hours dreaming, still as the stopped clock on the kitchen wall.

At school we prayed for years on end, our combined hail-marys and ourfathers amassed to millions. Prayer is a quantitative thing, subject to divine accountancy. God is a miser hoarding, hoarding, implacable. Our days were marked and divided by prayers and they soothed the hours that ebbed away into the darkness of the dormitory. Prayers like bandages. I never thought deeply about the words I intoned, or found mass anything more than a shuffling ritual, yet some might have seen me as devout, for when we prayed I was never distracted. Routines have always absorbed me. They're comforting, an anaesthetic that frees your thoughts for reverie. My daydreams were harmless, yet I was intrigued by the nuns' blankness and what it concealed; the bodies under those cumbersome habits, the pasts they'd forsaken, the life of what they called '*la communauté*', going on all the time in a part of the building that was out of bounds to us.

On Saturdays we went for long walks, with the nuns sweeping along in front and behind, in pairs just like us. Their movements in procession were those of automata, too disciplined to be graceful, even though at other times certain individuals among them had all the gliding smoothness of swans. Black swans, their dark feathers a prison for the spellbound daughters of a king.

One Sunday a month my mother came with a pink-iced cake she'd have made and other small packages carried in a net shopping bag. She would have got a taxi from the station, and since there was nowhere nearby for us to go for tea, we'd sit in one of the parlours along the ground-floor corridor. Four brown upholstered easy chairs and a low table were over-looked by a framed photograph of the Pope and a statue of Our Lady of Lourdes on a square shelf attached to the wall by a metal bracket. A squat candle burned in the red glass at her feet.

Oh, the boredom. But we set ourselves against it, wriggling and pushing to slough off that chrysalis of girlhood. We knew we were bound to escape, and fly off to become adults. It would end. And when all is said and done, in childhood the apparent permanence of things, the fact of what seems their eternal patterns, is not enough to make them entirely know-able. So much is witheld from us when we are young, and all institutions have a hidden set of rules and reasons. I attribute the success of my hotel in part to people's fascination with the enigmas of buildings whose organisation depends on invisible systems; things that only become secrets because they are unobtrusive. For some people the pursuit of anonymity kin-dles the very curiosity about others that they imagine must be directed towards themselves. And for them anonymous rooms harbour untold mysteries.

My over-pious education left me high and dry when it came to measuring the talents I would need for the future – a future as yet without the promise of marriage. Time enough for that, I thought. First I would test my wings. London, at that time a city where youth held sway, disappointed me. Had I been young a dozen years earlier, my class would have guar-anteed me a place in society that I might even have enjoyed.

Now such things were more haphazard. Now and then a gold-edged white card would drop through the letter-box and I would place it on the mantelpiece. But I did not belong at those parties, where the girls, jolly and good-natured, angled for dinner invitations from young men uncomfortable in cravats.

I had hoped for some excitement. The job my father had found for me through a family friend was dusty, cheerless work. The unvarying legal circumlocutions became a mono-tone in my head; I carried it with me into sleep. For reasons of economy, I lived in my parents' *pied à terre* in Wimpole Street. Alone, except when they, or, more usually, my father unaccompanied, came to London for the evening. This wasn't often, but my father had a habit of turning up unannounced after a dinner at his club. He would collapse in an armchair and fall asleep.

This flat was a basement, but its rooms were large and high-ceilinged, which made the few items of shabby furniture seem all the more misplaced. In the room at the front two spare beds stood either side of the grand fireplace, looking miniature, like babies' cots. In daylight, when I could no longer bear to see the passing procession of legs beyond the pavement railings, I would close the curtains.

If my father arrived on a Saturday night we would go to Sunday morning mass together. At other times I would follow my own inclinations, perhaps attending one Sunday in four. A habit it seemed as well not to let go of. It never crossed my mind to give up; lapsing would be an ostentatious and un-necessary gesture to myself. For variety's sake I chose a different church on each occasion. This was how I came to know something of London's different local populations, rich and poor.

I chose always to sit by the aisle, near the front. This way I watched people file past and return from Communion. The host, the fathers of the Church believed, nourished the body as well as the soul, with instantaneous effects on well-being. I was curious to see how far this worked; how the more ill-clad and pasty-faced of the communicants fared as they returned to their places, palms flat together, replenished by the wafer. And the others: did they shine with unaccustomed grace? Were their souls more substantial, now that they were cleansed and fed with the Sacrament? Yes, it's true, I made class distinctions, body *or* spirit, but it seems to me that people have to eat first before the blessings of the spirit can be enjoyed.

I myself underwent no transformations, bodily or other-wise, but I still sought them in others. You may think there was something dishonest in my stance of the watcher, but I meant no disrespect, I meant no mischief. I was wavering about who I was and could only watch others to see who I wasn't.

It was one Sunday morning after 9 o'clock mass at St Peter's that I spoke to my father about my longing to escape. I didn't put it in those words; even then I had the tact not to reveal too much dissatisfaction. As we sat breakfasting under the glare of an unshaded electric bulb in the windowless kitchen, I felt more than usually oppressed by my dismal sur-roundings. My youth was passing me by, unrecognised and unrequited by either the charm or the recklessness which was its due. But I told my father none of this, only that I'd been thinking that a stay in Paris would improve my French (the one advantage of my convent education). I would study, I said, and perhaps give English conversation classes, so that I needn't depend on remittances from home.

To my surprise, my father agreed that the idea was a good one. He insisted, however, that proper arrangements be made. There was no question of my becoming an *au pair* (something I hadn't myself considered); he and my mother would want to see me installed in a respectable household. My moral welfare mattered much more than economies. Of course they would support me, even if it meant sacrifices.

The outcome was speedier than I could have hoped. Through an old friend of my aunt's my mother found a solution. I was to have board and lodging in exchange for my services as a 'lady's companion'. My mother raised a finger and with it emphasised this point: in her young day such a position would have been unthinkable for a girl of my class – things had changed enough for my status in Madame Baillon's house not to suggest I'd come down in the world. As if to prove the fact she took me shopping. My wardrobe would be taken as proof of my origins, and so everything was bought at Jaeger.

As the taxi-driver unloaded my luggage, I stood on the pavement of Avenue Hoche and smoothed my coat, already conscious of perhaps being in view of those awaiting my arrival. I went on standing there, not because of nervousness or uncertainty, but because my journey was nearly over and I wished for a moment or two to prolong it. It was a Tuesday afternoon, early in autumn, and the light cast that rich melancholy glow that makes the lingering end of summer so full of glory. Cities, even countries, have their seasons, and this moment of arrival struck me as perfection. Spring is the season of departures, of cutting loose, of putting an end to what has lasted the winter and become stale. Autumn is the time for a new permanence, for an arrival at the end of wandering, and this was my first chosen city.

The concierge looked me over, taking in every detail of my dishevelment: my clothes, that I was now beginning to feel too hot in; my ringless hands. As if, I felt, she were checking a version she'd already had of me. Her husband took my two suitcases and I was struggling behind him with the rest of my things when we almost collided with a tall woman coming down the stairs. She pushed past the man and, seizing a holdall from my hand, addressed herself to me with what seemed a reproach. She spoke so quickly that I understood no more than this.

My first thought was that I had brought too much luggage; I had packed everything I owned, for what had been agreed as a six-month stay. Then, as I entered the salon, I heard a dry thin voice say in perfect English, 'Cécile would have arranged for you to be met at the station had you told us you were coming alone.'

Since I had been expected alone this puzzled me so much I was lost for an answer and stood for a moment, tongue-tied, my gaze fixed on the Turkish carpet that spread around me, before stretching out my hand to reach hers. Of course, they must have thought I'd be accompanied on the journey by my parents, or one of them at least.

Madame Baillon was a widow in her late sixties, arthritic and therefore partly immobilised. Her manner too was stiff, although always courteous. One of my duties was to help her with correspondence in English, which was often to do with her late husband's scholarly work (he had been a geologist and had published widely on his findings). I was to accompany her on errands (although her outings were rare), and take the dog for daily walks. I was also to be attentive to Madame's needs; an implicit part of the contract which was seen as just a matter of good manners. So I poured her coffee and her wine, adjusted the television and the radio as required, saw to the niceties of tea at five and, as my French improved, read to her from the newspaper when called upon.

In the afternoons Madame retired to her room and I was at liberty to go out. Otherwise it was a dull life, but that didn't bother me. It was, I knew, only the first stage in my new future. And, for the first time, I ate well; at Madame's table no one did penance, devout though she was. On Sundays I went with her to mass. It was a neighbourhood where worship was dignified and made fashionable by the existence of a number of churches serving emigré communities. There was the Russian Church and the English Catholic Church, and since churches and their congregations had a particular fascination for me I took this as an omen of my rightness there. I would visit them sometimes in the early morning, before breakfast, and watch people come and go.

The dog was to be walked before lunch and again before dinner. It was an airedale called Pierrot, good-natured enough, and I didn't mind the chore. In fact I thought we must have looked well-matched together: me in my smart rust-coloured coat of cashmere and wool, and he with his rough, wiry one of a similar hue, as if he were my dog and I

not just a borrowed mistress. We walked in the Parc Monceau.
I liked the sound of the Angelus bells as we made our
way back.

One day at lunch Madame told me this park had been a
favourite place of Marie Antoinette and that she was reputed
to have been there as the Bastille was being stormed. At that
time it had been filled with the exotic simulations of which
the court was so fond: pagodas and a willow-pattern bridge,
an Egyptian pyramid and a Roman temple.

Madame spoke about it almost wistfully, as if she herself
remembered. 'And, you know, mademoiselle,' she concluded,
'this garden was the work of a landscape architect so proud of
its artificiality that he put up a sign that said THIS IS NOT AN
ENGLISH GARDEN.'

It was Madame's style to tell me lunch-table anecdotes that
had some pedagogical kernel. Perhaps something of her husband's ghost animated this desire to educate me. She herself,
it seemed, had never been anything other than his wife, and
now lived in his immortal shadow.

I came to suspect that everything there had been preserved
just as he had left it. Dusted, but untouched by any hands,
hardly even looked at. Along the dark corridor geological
specimens sat in deep glass cases between ceiling-high shelves
that held thousands of books on many different subjects.

Every Thursday, an old friend of the family came to tea.
Madame told me I could extend my freedom by one hour on
these afternoons, if I wished. Then, one Thursday, with the
extreme courtesy I had by now learned to read as a code of
command, she asked me to return in time to have tea with her

and Monsieur Maréchal, who had expressed a desire to make my acquaintance.

He was a charming man, slender, nimble and bright eyed. The skin of his face was pale, but with a rosy translucence, as if some inner pinkness of good health shone through; and although wrinkled round the eyes, it was smooth elsewhere, an effect of ageing quite the opposite of Madame's withered complexion. One thing repelled me, though: the sour meaty odour that came from his mouth when he leant towards me, teacup in hand, for a cube of sugar to be dropped from the tongs. This made me think of zoos and circuses, the rank sawdust smell they have; and especially of lions and lion-tamers.

Monsieur Maréchal was a painter; not entirely an amateur, for at forty he had handed over the family business to his younger brother to devote himself to art and travel. He asked if I would like to see his work and, since Madame showed no sign of disapproving, I gave an enthusiastic answer. As he left, he turned and handed me his card: '*Venez demain, si vous voulez, à trois heures.*'

I was prompt. The maid showed me into a long room that at the far end was furnished with all the comforts of a salon while half its area had the appearance of a studio. A pair of floor-length windows overlooked the Parc Monceau. She gestured towards a red velvet sofa. From this vantage point I looked down across the trees and the paths where figures walked silently.

I turned as he entered the room, followed by the maid bearing a tray which was placed on a small round table between the windows. 'You'll drink a glass of Malaga wine, I hope.' By now the glasses were full and I could only accept. The sweet raisiny taste on my tongue and the thickly sliced sponge cake that came with the wine made me feel like a child who was being entertained. 'Mademoiselle, it is kind of you to visit me. I have often watched you down there in the park and hoped that we should meet. You walk gracefully when you are alone.'

Of course, he'd known who I was because of the dog. Now he was drawing my attention to the paintings on the wall behind me. Some were views of the park, or rather the same view, through the windows, but in different lights and seasons. In others the sun bore down from fiery skies on to vermilion blossoms and the rampant green of spiked and feathered foliage. The south, I thought, or maybe somewhere further. And they were beautiful, in a way that disturbed me, for these paintings too seemed to capture the same scene, over and over, though with more dramatic variations that gave them the quality of an obsession.

I knew too little to ask the right questions, so I kept silent, but my host seemed satisfied with my response – to which he had been closely attentive.

Then he showed me the masks and the wood carvings he had collected on his travels – 'the whole world'; and his thin little arms made as if to embrace it. The gods of the Pacific, of North and West Africa, or Mexico and Guatemala looked down on us from a high frieze across one wall. Beneath them were portraits and figures, some of them nudes. 'Not all of these are mine, just a few; but now that I am old I paint more people, and fewer landscapes. I no longer travel, you see.'

When he asked if I would mind sitting for him I wasn't

surprised, but this didn't prevent my embarrassment showing. The intimacy of the request was too sudden. Yet I agreed without further hesitation after his tactful assurance that I was to pose as I was: 'in this same blue pullover and dark skirt that so become you'. Then he asked if I would mind one thing, if I would take off my shoes and stockings, for he very much wanted to paint my feet.

And so I crept barefoot from behind a small screen, feeling the chill of the floor around the Persian rug. My chair was dull red leather and high-backed, with arms I was not to lean on. I was unaccustomed to posing. I didn't know how to relax my limbs and on that first day I soon became stiff and uncomfortable. After that, though, the sessions were short, he encouraged me to stop every now and then. I would get up and move around, and he would watch me with a tight, assessing gaze that made me want simultaneously to command his admiration and to run away far out of his sight. When I returned to my place he would rearrange my limbs.

His hands were always cold, but not unpleasantly so.

We begin every session with the Malaga wine and the thick-cut cake, served to me once I am barefoot and in my chair. While I am posing, at least once he will rise and step towards me, making a slight but insistent gesture that says I am not to move, not to disturb the pose. Then he'll stop, a few feet away, the distance always the same, as if preordained, and, tilting his head, inflecting his chin, pursing his lips a little, he examines me inch by inch with his eyes. Every curve and angle of me, every proportion, as if I am being mapped, measured in sections and memorised by heart.

After a minute or two of this he'll describe a circle around me, slowly, almost warily. And now I feel like a statue, all the lines of my body frozen, the liquid drape of my clothes turned solid, petrified by his glance. 'Don't move your eyes!' he snaps, when once I try to follow the path of his vision. And I obey, persuading myself that this surrender is a part of any sitter's pact, however perilous. At the twelve o'clock position, he stops again, directly behind me, and stays there for just as long as he has stood in front of me. This is very strange, since he can see nothing of me, or maybe just the crown of my head above the chair's high back. He stands, so still, his breathing so audibly even, that I can tell he is rooted to the spot, perhaps as motionless as me. But for what? I cannot fathom. Nor can I be sure that there is not some perfectly simple explanation for this encirclement. Perhaps something merely to do with the artist exercising his eye, judging the relationships of planes and perspectives. I dare not ask.

But once he comes into view again, I feel a release from something. I observe his tread, my eyes downcast – as they are meant to be – and resting on the highly polished toes of his shoes that now turn away from me back to where he was before, safe beside the easel. The silent cracking of the whip has ceased. Silent, or perhaps existing just in my imagination.

After two weeks and six visits in all I asked how much longer the painting would take and was glad when Monsieur Maréchal told me it would be some time yet, perhaps a few more weeks. I knew then how much I liked to pose, how much I relished our shared rituals, even the harmless secrecy that had been established; for on the first day Monsieur had said it was perhaps best not to tell Madame Baillon about the painting. She had certain ideas about decorum that were undoubtedly old-fashioned and he preferred not to trouble her.

Her husband had had a very different character, he told me: a man of great learning, open to ideas. Madame's husband, whom he spoke of as a great friend he missed very much, came into Sylvain Maréchal's conversation on a number of occasions. One afternoon he asked if I had made any use of the library in Madame's flat. He told me I would be surprised by what I should find if I looked on the top shelf in the corridor, just outside my room.

That night, before going to bed, I took my bedside chair and, standing on it, reached up for the topmost row of books, pulling them out one by one to read the titles. I remembered the forbidden high shelves in the library at school, forbidden to all but the senior girls, and how, when my turn came, I had wondered at the reasons for their prohibition. There had been nothing to shock among the George Orwells and the Aldous Huxleys; only the horrors of Room 101.

Here, however, there was no disappointment. These were antiquarian books, dating, it seemed to me, from the eighteenth century, finely bound and printed on thick, rough-edged paper. They were bulky and unwieldy and I dared not keep even one of them in my room, where it might be noticed, or leave a tell-tale gap on the shelf. After perusal I returned them there, and then decided to borrow a small, almost miniature volume which surely wouldn't be missed — a short novel of sorts whose chapters were each preceded by a plate showing a lewd bedroom scene.

By modern standards of beauty, the women were fat, monstrously pear-shaped. Skirts were pulled up from behind to show buttocks and thighs that were soft balloons of flesh; neat waists and prettily dimpled arms compounded this grotesqueness, while the leering men in whose embraces they made a pretence of struggle looked ready to overbalance under the weight of their giant phalluses. And yet even these comic incongruities turned my throat dry and I made impatient efforts to read the faded print. Over and over again, the trusting heroine is duped into sexual subservience. She makes only the feeblest protests and the smallest attempts to escape her lustful tormentors. Innocent and pliable, she merely floats in the wash of what happens to her. Surrounded by the dark stillness of Madame Baillon's flat and filled with the knowledge of my transgression, I found a thrill of new pleasure. Why, some of the villains were priests.

Next morning I had no chance to return the book to its place so I hid it in my bedroom cupboard under some towels. I began then to wonder at Monsieur's motives in guiding me towards such literature – and at my role as demure barefoot muse. Suddenly uneasy, I chose to stay away from that day's session. It was Tuesday; I went to the Louvre instead and got back just in time for tea.

As I was pouring our second cups, Cécile came in looking rather flustered. She'd forgotten to say, but Monsieur Maréchal had telephoned for me. I'd been out and Madame was taking her nap. Perhaps I looked guilty; Madame's raised eyebrows compelled some explanation. I'd met Monsieur in the park the other day and he'd mentioned a young acquaintance who wanted lessons in English conversation.

No sooner was the lie out of my mouth than I regretted it and saw its foolishness. I shrugged. Madame maintained her air of perplexity. I saw then that some discourtesy had taken place.

'Monsieur didn't ask to speak to me?' she queried, without looking at Cécile, and smoothing the edge of the tablecloth where the cake-stand had made a crease.

'No, Madame,' Cécile answered, her hands falling to adjust this lapse.

As if relieved, Madame raised her eyes to mine and gave me an abrupt smile.

'Then you must return Monsieur's call as soon as we have finished tea.'

Of course by now I feared he would ring again and anxiety chipped away at my concentration. Madame could not but have noticed my halting responses to her conversation.

'I've just been given your message,' I blurted, the telephone receiver at last safe in my hand. There was a pause, then, 'How kind of you to telephone, Mademoiselle.' The words seemed less an answer to mine than an avoidance of confirmation. Had he telephoned? I was confused by the possibility that Cécile had somehow misunderstood. 'Well then,' he continued, 'come tomorrow at three o'clock – *si vous voulez*.'

Now I dared not stay away. I'd hung a cloud of guilt around myself and feared Monsieur's betrayal; even though it was he who had insisted on secrecy.

Everything in the room was as always. It was my own presence there that was different, reluctant and yet a little excited by uncertainty. The tray sat ready, the ruby-filled decanter encircled by a dull gleam of silver, the sponge cake a deep mango-yellow. A bowl of green apples held curves of sunlight by Monsieur's elbow. He rose to greet me, smiling and shaking his small head as if lamenting and simultaneously forgiving my absence. I went behind the screen, removed my shoes and stockings and took my usual place in the chair. He handed me a glass and I sipped in silence. We both did. Monsieur dipped a finger of Madeira in his wine, bit on it with a delicate sucking motion, then asked me the question I had been half-expecting ever since I had first come to his studio.

'Mademoiselle, I have a request. You may say no, of course, if you wish. I would like to make a sketch of your breasts. It will, I'm sure, help my painting of you to be better.' He lifted a heavy block of paper from the table beside him and gestured towards the screen. I was to return behind it and remove more of my clothes.

I doubted my responses: indignation, fear of seeming merely prudish. Monsieur was a real painter and such requests were commonplace for models, although – I waited for him to release me from what I'd now come to understand as an order. But he only smiled, and, as if I had no choice, I did as he asked. Yet I had a choice. I could have dressed and left the room, ignoring the veiled, perhaps playful threats he had made. No, it wasn't only this shadow of guilt that kept me there. I belonged. I'd become a part of the room. Like the other objects in it, I'd been chosen. Here, I could look at myself with pride, even if through someone else's eyes.

It was as a coquette that I returned to my chair, determined to demonstrate the refusal of any intended humiliation. To my astonishment I saw that the cheval mirror had been wheeled out of the corner and placed at an angle that enabled Monsieur to see my reflection as he drew, but also made my image inescapable for my own eyes. I had a boyish figure, pale, thin shouldered, my dark skirt loose at my waist; and now in the mirror I mocked myself for it.

Monsieur drew. Perhaps fifteen minutes passed. Then the doorbell and the commotion in the hall. Madame Baillon's voice made my heart turn over and before I could move, take cover, both leaves of the door were flung open and she burst into the room. She stopped in her tracks when she saw me. A sharp intake of breath, then she lurched forward as if to seize me by the arm, but the rug slipped beneath her and she fell, her lost crutch flying against the mirror with a crack. It was a curious scene, frozen in my memory into a single moment, into a tableau of onlookers around a central moving figure whose face was twisted with pain.

After that, there was no question of my remaining Madame Baillon's guest. If my misdemeanours alone had not been enough to banish me, Madame's indignity on the studio floor had sealed my fate. The discovery of my illicit reading had no doubt provoked the sortie to Monsieur's house. Yet behind all these trivial circumstances that had combined to secure my expulsion, I had an obscure sense of conspiracy. As if everything had been a pretext and I a victim.

If I was, I did not remain one. Despite those awkward beginnings, I have made my way in life and made Paris my home. In some way they helped, though I did not undertake the life of vice to which Madame asserted I was prone in the letter my parents received from her. I smoothed things over on the telephone, but they demanded my return and refused to support me if I stayed on.

And there begins my story. For I had to earn money. I rented the cheapest room I could find: an attic with only a small sink to wash in and a Turkish toilet in the corridor. I bought a primus stove and cooked vegetables on it. My mattress swallowed most of the space. I was there for two years.

What gave me courage was the view from my window. Rooftops frosted over in the early mornings and at night gilded by sunset, lit by flickers of neon from the dark cliffs below. I learned the ruthlessness of the lonely, those who belong nowhere except in places of their own making. I worked hard, modelling at Beaux Arts, giving English lessons, guiding tourists round the city with a paper parasol in my hand as a beacon for the stragglers. Later, I was offered a job in one of the grand hotels, in the ranks of the superior staff. All the time I was saving, then a small inheritance at last brought my dream to reality.

Now, the view from my windows is not so different from those early days, but I've become mistress of what I survey, for I know this city and all those on the three floors below my apartment conduct themselves in the knowledge of my presence.

It's a hotel, but not just a hotel. This is, and always has been, a city of debauched dreams, as well as being the spring-time metropolis where the world's spirits lift. Those who cross my threshold want a reminder of that, a reminder and maybe something more. They too play their part. They notice everything.

Decor is one of the things they pay for. Nothing too

obvious, nor vulgar, but sometimes a touch out of place – like the holy picture on the bedroom walls: the Sacred Heart; Our Lady of Perpetual Succour; Saint Thérèse, both of them: the Little Flower and the other with her grimace of ecstasy . . . The usual pantheon, and a few intriguing unknowns. Paper saints are unshockable and in the constant company of those who sin they become indulgent.

Each room has a few erotic scenes on the walls; tasteful for the most part, things that I've picked up at the auction halls. A few miniatures, some humorous sketches. Some good reproductions of fine art works too; one I'm particularly fond of is Boucher's painting of Louise O'Murphy's Foot. I have it in my parlour.

My rooms are like hotel rooms everywhere, yet they are all unique. Their moods and colours vary: lurid, sombre, roseate, verdant, funereal. Some are perfumed; lilac or mimosa, jasmine from the south; one or two even have an odour of sanctity that comes from incense and dripping candle wax. Fragrances have an afterlife that quickens the memory, poignant, as everyone knows. Accusatory fragrances for those who come here looking for guilt to follow them. I see to it, they imagine, though it's a matter of chance in most cases.

I don't claim to possess great insight into human nature. I'm no psychologist, yet I'm credited with the power to discern the recesses of their desires, so I'm told. Whatever they come for, with their lovers and mistresses, their bosses and secretaries and who knows what other illicit combinations (even husbands and wives, I daresay) what I give them is theatrical enough to stir a few fantasies, that's all.

Rooms conducive to dreams, I call them; that's what it

says at the bottom of the staircase. A discreet motto, it's the first thing they see when they arrive. But I make them wait. A little ritual no one is allowed to break. As their reservations are checked, on the pretence of some last-minute arrangements, they're invited to have a drink in my ground-floor parlour. Drinks are on the house of course, but should they refuse they're likely to be told there's some mistake or confusion that lets them down flat . . . we'll see what we can do, however, if you'll just take a seat in the parlour . . .

That kind of firm hospitality lets people know who's in charge. First-timers at the hotel sometimes find the maid service a little disconcerting too. After the rooms are cleaned guests may well find things moved, pictures changed around or replaced, and instead of that universal tidying which indiscriminately gathers objects into neat little bedside regiments – piles of coins and house keys, nail-files and lipstick, passports and receipts – my chambermaids will have scattered and hidden things of this kind in odd corners of the room. A perfume bottle perched on top of the wardrobe, keys buried under a pillow, a discarded dress draped on a hanger and slung over the shower curtain rail, a shoe stepped into the washbasin.

Of course, it is not unusual for people to suspect they're being watched, even to convince themselves that the wall mirrors are two-way (it's happened more than once that a maid has found something draped over these). Some are deterred from a second visit, but the fact is I have regulars and my establishment is a success.

Me? Well, I can honestly say the years have treated me well. I was never a beauty, but I had something that worked with men, something that has outlasted my youth. I have no shortage of lovers; they come and go and are soon replaced. Some leave of their own accord, others bore me to the point where I have to make it plain they're no longer welcome. No hard feelings, I say.

I'm busy, but when I have time I might drive over to the Parc Monceau and take a walk there alone. I'm fond, too, of the Buttes Chaumont, fond of its romantic artificiality, the craggy rocks and rustic railings made of concrete and now so weathered and worn with time they might just as well be the real thing. It's a place where anyone can feel at home.

And there's a little hobby I have, a little mania, as the French say.

Paris is not the best place for astronomy, but a few years ago I bought a telescope. On especially clear nights I sit with it at the attic window. I can gaze for hours at a star or two.

Crossing the Line

Our house had a radar panel on the roof, a humming rod revolving silver in the sun. But the summers were short and for most of the year the wind ripped around us from the open sea. My mother's laundry on the line was my idea of sails and rigging; there were always sheets and tablecloths out there, pulling tension in the crisscrossed ropes that stretched a triangle over our patch of garden. A line of trees bordering the cliff path gave me weather clues in the morning. My bedroom was sheltered from the precipice and the window framed a tall silver birch that shook and was bent and bowed with such extravagance I was always convinced this would be the day the wind tore it out or pushed it to fall beneath its own weight. In stillness it looked twisted and disabled.

My father was the coastguard. I know he drank sometimes and would sleep it off wrapped in a blanket by the kitchen range. But he worked hard. My mother did too. We took all her time, we children *and my grandmother, who was sick. My mother was thin and the pale colour of her eyes might have been from tiredness; were they ever darker?*

At night I read stories under the covers with a torch, and dreamed myself at sea. Everything from that time is coloured by water and sky, ocean depths and rain. And ships. Pointing towards some far-off sunny harbour. Valparaiso maybe.

It's spring now, a green vase on the table, the quivering blue irises rearing their dragon heads against the sea window where I sit, looking out. There's a story I could tell about a woman who went to sea.

Kathy Bell met Gerry McGlone one October when she was leaving her receptionist's job to join Cunard. 'Have a drink with me, Kate,' he said, with a teasing look, and she laughed too, for she'd admired him long before he'd spoken to her, and she thought he knew it.

He drank whisky; she had tomato juice. There was fever in her cheeks all the same. Afterwards they went to see a Humphrey Bogart film. Walking home, she took his arm, her fingers wanting to smooth the serge, to touch every button, every inch of braid. She was sure as she needed to be that he was the one she would marry. Gerry and Kate, she said to herself.

Luck gave them an engagement present of a first voyage together. Entering the straits of Gibraltar, the ship sounded its horn, and Kate, clearing a tea-tray from a cabin, looked out and saw the Rock, still small in the distance, so hazy and sea-washed, so unlikely it might be a mirage, like the ones she had heard of on the west coast of Africa. Her first sight of the Mediterranean brought her, in a rush of surprise, to a recognition of herself, as if she were approaching not just Gibraltar, but the destination of her life: a port and a husband. Everything had been leading to this. That night they went dancing.

They were married at home in Glasgow, at St Luke's. Her friend Helen Sweeney was her bridesmaid, in pink, and her sister's eldest girl, Joanne, carried a silver horseshoe she was meant to give to the bride, and dropped in a puddle. All Kate's family were there and Gerry's two brothers. His mother was too frail to travel, but Kate met her in Dublin on the honeymoon, after they'd spent a week in Warrenpoint. She'd have liked to visit her childhood haunts in the west, but there wasn't time for the journey.

After that she had little choice but to be a purser's fireside wife. The loneliness came as a bitter shock.

In the evenings, unless someone dropped in, or she went to see her mother, she had only the wireless for company. On the winter mornings, knocking the ashes from the grate, she shivered from solitude as much as from the early chill. Night brought a physical ache when the dark tantalised her with memories of touch. Her body felt wasted. It made her curse the cruise ships.

She was pregnant by Gerry's first shore-leave. Two kinds of waiting then. When she had him in her arms, she knew this was the cure, this day and night stealing baby, his eyes in a blue trance, the last liquid signs from the liquid world he'd inhabited inside her. Gerry and Kate and Peter.

When Peter was two, in 1953, she had another baby. She craved babies. How else could she fill the months of separation, or have Gerry with her when he was out at sea?

Joseph cried more than Peter; he was a demanding infant, showing off his lung power, already a roaring boy, which pleased his dad. Kate let Gerry sleep, for he needed his rest on shore, and she got up in the night to see to the baby.

Her mother had died a month before Joseph's birth and more than ever she had need of a family around her. But Gerry's homecomings made her restless, drawing her out of the sleepy milkiness of motherlove and making her look in the mirror again. At these times she saw how much the children wore her out and made her absent from herself. When Gerry was due in she had her hair done, after taking the children to her sister's and having a bath there. The bathroom, all scented luxury, was her only envy of Valerie. When they moved and had one too, she would fill it with globe-stoppered jars of pink crystals and puffers of perfumed talcum powder and ducks and inflatable balls for the kids.

Gerry would arrive to find her stretched long-legged on the settee, her full skirt spreading patterned print roses or taffeta shimmers wide across it. There would be a big all-night-lasting fire, and music, the bottle and glasses and sandwiches ready, and the children sound asleep. It was how she planned it, to be there just for him, the princess waiting for her prince.

There was an afterthought of disappointment if he turned up in the morning instead, finding her in the mess and muddle of the kids.

With Gerry away, she was marooned. Nappies drying on the fireguard, steam rising from the hearth, fanning the smell of toast and scalded milk. Neighbours helped out, so did Valerie and the nieces and Helen Sweeney, but she felt like a fixed point in everyone else's firmament – always there. People strayed into her family circle because it was so often incomplete. Mrs Torrance from next door chapped on the window most days and asked if she needed anything and more often than not it was her daughter Marguerite who went to the shops.

Kate made tea, 'baby tea' for Marguerite, who wrinkled up her nose at all the milk in it, but her smile escaped when she saw the chocolate biscuits. She was shy, with lowered dark eyes that watched the children; curious, maybe even envious. Never cuddling or fussing over them the way girls of her age did usually. Sometimes, after long silences, she relayed back-court gossip, but as if wanting Kate's verdict in return. 'My mammy says Mrs Gallagher makes her tea with the water she boils her egg in.'

'Does she?'

Marguerite wasn't her real name. She'd picked it herself, 'out of a book', but it suited her better than Margaret. She'd paid for it with ridicule at home and mockery at school. Two girls shadowed her from the bus-stop now, snorting and giggling as they chanted 'Marguerite, tweet-tweet'.

Peter was five and Joe three when Gerry came back for a longer leave after several bouts of sickness. He was told to cut down his drinking. Or else. She worried but was glad at the thought of him there for the birth of their third child.

'You're not a real man till you've fathered a daughter, Gerry,' claimed his brother Phil, loud in roguish admiration.

Sylvia Mary had a doll face with long lashes and her gossamer hair was copper coloured. Kate hoped it would stay that way, not darken as hers had. As she nursed her, mother and daughter gazed at one another saucer-eyed in disbelief. Gerry recovered.

For two more years he kept his job. His health would flag, then he would seem to get well. One wet February night there was a faint ring at the door; when she opened it he collapsed in her arms, his case and kitbag clattering down the steps. He had a temperature of 104. The doctor came within the hour. He said it was best not to move him, so Kate arranged for Sylvia Mary and Joe to stay at Valerie's. They were brought home after a week because Gerry wanted them there. Mrs Torrance took them for odd spells in the day while Kate nursed Gerry.

Gerry died. 'You know it was his liver.' The doctor's tone made Kate frown back at him.

He had died in their double bed, with her gripping his hand, their fingers enlaced with a rosary blessed in Lourdes. Her first gesture was to throw the rosary away. She found it, weeks later, under the bed, the pearlised beads glinting at her, and it put her in a rage again. She suffered from rage all the more now that she no longer gave way to tears; crying exhausted her and the children would start crying too.

Still, her life with Gerry seemed, looking back, the way it was meant to be, and his death a part of it. She knew he could have saved himself, but that wasn't how he was. Their marriage had been happy, passionate to the end. He'd thought the world of her, spoiled her with presents and intemperate love; but if he hadn't been at sea, they'd have fought like cat and dog. The sea and the whisky had swallowed his wildness and left the sweetness for her.

When she faced the future she saw a lifetime of quiet evenings. She hadn't minded them while she was waiting; there was always saved-up life to be lived once Gerry walked in through the door. She would never remarry. Yet a lifetime of quiet evenings wouldn't be enough. Her children going short of the things other kids had. Never moving from these two rooms.

Gerry had been a spender. But some money was left in the bank, the Post Office account, the title deeds. This solved nothing.

Six weeks after the funeral she got a job in a Sauchiehall Street department store. Valerie took Sylvia Mary and picked the boys up from school every day. She sold gloves and hosiery until they switched her to one of the beauty counters by the ground-floor entrance, a temporary replacement for what they called an 'estetician'. They told her to wear more make-up. Her legs ached from standing all day in stilettos and her lips were dry and tight from powder-caked lipstick and reluctant smiling. Cold air gusted past her whenever a customer came in or went out.

Guilty as a plotter, she sat down one night after doing the dishes and wrote the letter.

There was nothing she had not foreseen in her sister's gentle fury. She also knew it would abate; she was counting on it.

The company man who'd inquired about arrangements for the children had been persuaded by her calm assurance about the boarding-school chosen for the boys and her sister's willingness to make a home for Sylvia Mary. A friend of Gerry's had helped, but charm had got her the job. For the first time in her life she was using it purposefully. A smile and a handshake. 'You've got the right sort of personality, Mrs McGlone.'

Gerry's brothers came round and bawled her out. They didn't speak to her again for nearly two years. Valerie defended her.

She admitted it was all a gamble. She would give it a year. By then, she would have spent the savings anyway. Eking out was something she'd had no practice in.

The boys would have each other.

'They'll be mixing with the better off.'

'They'll be looked down on.'

She had thought about all that. They were clever at school. Joe could hold his corner even with the bigger kids and Peter had the gift of making people laugh to make up for his fragility. 'There's nobody any better than you.' It was simple because she honestly believed it, so they believed it too.

Seeing the name tags she'd sewn on their grey shirts, their blazers and gabardine coats, adding these to the pile of identical clothes to be packed in their trunks, she thought that by resembling the other children in every detail, they would be made equal. Every item on the school's long list, winter and summer, was there. On day one though, walking from the school to the station, registering the blur of the other parents' passing cars, flinching still from Peter's look of reproach and Joe's sudden tears as she left them, she wondered, for the first time, if she'd made an awful mistake, and was at once appalled by the vision of her ruthlessness.

Others saw folly. But admiration, as well as disapproval, came from unlikely quarters. No one could suspect her of not loving her children.

She herself had all she needed. An off-duty wardrobe that was more than adequate for warmer climates, a use now for all Gerry's oriental spoils. Silk blouses wrapped in tissue paper and still unworn, a shantung two-piece he'd had made overnight in Hong Kong. Even silk pyjamas. She would be in uniform mostly. Her pay would reach the bank untouched. Cruise passengers were heavy tippers. This had entered her calculations.

On her first voyage there was another stewardess called Kate. Being Kathy again avoided confusion. The old name stuck. Kathy was new-born, cut loose from children and recriminations. She had left mourning behind too. Grief, attenuated in the months before, still echoed in her sleep, but her waking hours were claimed by thoughts of other absences, by energies seized to solve the future. Things she hadn't known would be possible.

The letters and cards she wrote to Valerie sounded the triumph of distance. Distance had even more glamour in those days, just before cheap package holidays set millions in motion towards the sun. Valerie, married to an accountant, was not immune to the romance of travel. Her collection of shells, laid out with a geometry governed by size and species on the middle shelves of the living-room alcove, had been started with what Gerry had brought from his trips. Kate would bring her shells too. Now, viewing the hillside skyscrapers of Montreal, the whitewashed cube houses huddled on the slopes of Lindos, the pale hanks of palm-shaded Caribbean sand that came in the post, she experienced mild pangs of envy.

Kathy sent different cards to Sylvia Mary, and a whole sun-lit itinerary was mapped out on the wall above Valerie's Formica-topped kitchen table.

At first the boys sent strangled bulletins of their loneliness. This desperation urged her to return. In a fit of worry she resolved to give up the job; then, between letters, they showed signs of settling down. Uncomplaining news came, of games, friends, teachers, the gardener's dog. For all of them the miseries of separation softened and by her second leave six months later, her cases crammed with marvels to give, the reunion was happy and calm. They seemed to admire her now, adore her, the slender suntanned mother who wore lipstick all the time and earrings that flattered her broad-boned Irish face. It was the kind of face that was thought of as handsome.

In her children's adoration she observed hesitance, a missed beat in their words and their hugs. It wasn't estrangement, she thought, far from it, more like how they might have been with their dad. This withdrawal of neediness only hurt her a little.

When they parted at Glasgow Central, Peter asked her please not to mention her work in the postcards she sent them. The demands of deception were of her own making, and she promised. She had tried to give him a photograph of herself in uniform, but he hadn't wanted it.

She felt taller in her uniform. It defined her, made her more distinct, releasing her from a vague unease about herself that had troubled her since Gerry's death. She thrived on travel. She could see how passengers chose it as a means of obliterating past misfortune: widows and widowers, jilted fiancées. Secrets badly hidden at first would often vapourise on the voyage. Travel helped you forget who you were. Of course, you didn't forget who you were on a job with routines and responsibilities. That wasn't lotus-eating.

She mistrusted her doubleness, with an inchoate fear that Kathy would stop being Kate altogether, that the intoxication she felt each time the ship sailed would induce an insidious amnesia, that each voyage, with its landfall in another world, would erase a little more of memory, blurring the imprint of what she'd left behind.

She thought constantly of the children. She came to suspect that the blizzard of mail dispatched to them from port after port was less an insurance against them forgetting her than the other way round, an obsessive remembering. She posted cards to others, with something of the same insistence to herself. Only the ones she sent to young Marguerite Torrance were pure gifts, destined simply for the recipient. She could imagine Marguerite deciphering the postmarks, puzzling over the printed words in foreign languages, and much later pinning them on her bedroom wall beside the map of Europe above her bed.

These pictures of far away places would be a proof and a promise. For Marguerite geography was illicit, like so much else she daydreamed.

It had been not just the cynics who had believed Kathy's renewed career to be a man-chase. Here was a woman who wouldn't be long without a husband, and in the hunting-grounds of the cruise ships he would likely be a wealthy one. Her own motives were beyond the grasp of such reasoning.

She flirted and was flirted with. Nothing more. One night

when the band had played to a nearly empty ballroom crossing the Bay of Biscay in a force ten gale, and had wrapped up
early, she got to know a saxophonist called Mac Daly. He was
from Fyfe, a one-time candidate for the priesthood who had
got as far as the Scots college in Rome. There, he had lasted
six weeks. He had drifted for years.

This was her first affair, before or since Gerry's death. It was
consummated in Lisbon and ended in Alexandria.

She had liked being with him, but found his surface lightness too full of evasive ironies to be trusted. She told him so
with some small regret, remarking also that he drank too
much. He wasn't broken-hearted and her bluntness impressed
him. They got on well after that and she came to feel there
were times she could rely on him. The notoriously unreliable
sometimes single people out to contradict themselves, she
thought. Faith, but not need, drew them to others.

She was changing. When she went home she felt remote
from Valerie. She had to stop herself from saying certain
things: words, thoughts that must have been foreign to her
before. Her sister's concerns seemed improbable: perpetual
redecoration, Swedish place settings.

It wasn't just that she was enlarging the way she saw the
world. There was something odd about seeing it from the
deck of a ship, a floating palace that brushed against the edges
of countries and continents.

At first these took her breath away. The senses tuned in to
exoticism, so much abrupt and pungent newness. A deliver-
ance as you entered harbour. Occasional shocks of unlikely
familiarity; she'd got suddenly homesick in San Francisco,
whose steep streets had reminded her of Glasgow's dizzy

perspectives from Garnethill. Later, the accumulation of land-falls became a kind of taunting knowledge. Knowing how little you knew of what you saw, heard, touched, tasted.

Sea-changes. Circumnavigation did strange inward things to people. She'd met an engineer, a boy with an impish little face and pale, fringed hair. His slight build declared him too puny for the engine room until she noticed his hands, which were large and powerful, properly calloused and with grime-rimmed nails. They belonged on a different body, as, singly, did his eyes, unmatched, one blue, the other hazel. This angelic freakishness beguiled her. Seeing him alone and forlorn in the crew bar one night, she befriended him.

He had been two years at sea after working in a Tyneside shipyard. He had a girl at home, an engagement just before leaving. He still wrote to her and saw her on leaves, but too much had happened to him. India, the ragged poor sleeping on Calcutta streets, diseases suppurating through the teeming city. This much suffering was unholy, and it circled the world. He had never known this before. In Rio the poor live on the hills that rise above the city, because there is no water there; in Chittagong they live in the valley swamps and the rich inhabit the heights. Back in Sunderland he'd told these things to Linda and she'd listened. But then he couldn't kiss her, couldn't touch her. In the snapshot pulled from his wallet she had dark curly hair. She was keen to marry soon and have children. But he felt too tainted for physical love. What he'd wanted before didn't matter; he'd lost all relish for such paltry joys.

Kathy tried to persuade him otherwise, to give him heart. 'What will you do?'

'I have to do something. The sin is ignoring it.'

But she could see only futility and despair in him, the start of a future stony with guilt. Prayers and postal orders sent to charities.

He might be happier back on a merchant ship. Luxury was hideous, he said.

She noticed the onset of absent-mindedness; sometimes she would find herself lost in contemplation of a photograph or an object, intent on some detail. Her compulsion to remember had surrounded her with talismans. Among the snapshots and studio portraits of her clan, on her side of the shared cabin, she had hung a small painting bought in a Veracruz crafts shop. Its earth-coloured geometric patterns converged on a central eye that stared out at her, wide, unlidded, its pupil a brilliant lapis lazuli blue. Although it was Mexican and, she thought, traditional, it could have just as easily been Egyptian. She was gladdened by this. She had come to see such global kinships as matching pieces of a jigsaw. Resemblances prevailed.

She had become more of a reader. It was in a way how she got to know Jack Leaton, the man who proposed to her. Bringing him a late morning drink one day, she had offered to adjust his deck umbrella to block out the encroaching glare. It took a few minutes, fiddling with the catch, positioning it. He watched her all the time. She had seen him watching her before. Far beneath them algae swept the still surface of the Sargasso Sea. She saw the book on his drinks table was *A Burnt Out Case*, and, by way of the casually attentive conversation cruise passengers were used to, remarked that she liked Graham Greene and was this one good?

'You're welcome to borrow it; I've finished.' He held it out to her. His smile was knowing. It had puzzled her.

When they reached Antigua he asked her out to dinner. It was their first port of call in the Caribbean, and she accompanied him ashore at others. None of the men she had met after Gerry had moved her. She thought Jack might. She liked his steadiness, his firmness about everything. He had a face you would turn and look at in a crowd; the bushy, wriggling eyebrows gave it an air of energetic seriousness.

His family had been Lithuanian Jews who had started the clothing business he ran in Manchester. He'd built it up, he said, working all hours. He was convalescing from a road accident. Shock, a few fractures, then exhaustion catching up with him. After the rest on the crossing he longed for lively company, now that he was restored to life.

He brought up the subject of marriage in Kingston. He hadn't thought of remarrying until now. His divorce had soured him. This trip had allowed him to reflect, relax his emotions. He said he loved her.

She reflected too, on love, on what she still wanted from life. Didn't she want to be with her children, not just in the summer holidays, but always. And to give them the best of everything. Irreconcilables, without a chance like this.

It was over four years now. She was less sure. Not about replacing Gerry, but about marriage. And being in Manchester wouldn't matter, except there was Valerie.

But she wasn't ready yet. She wanted another year or two before settling down forever. She told him this in Miami, wishing it were somewhere else; she didn't like Miami. She wasn't sure why she gave him this answer. She thought if she had met him in her first year at sea it might have been different.

It seemed far away, that first year. She remembered crossing the line. The second steward had found out in advance which of the ratings were first-timers. The minor indignities they had had to undergo had reminded her of her cousin Bernadette's last day at work before her wedding. They'd pushed her in a wheelbarrow round the streets outside the warehouse, paint in her hair, lipstick streaked on her nose and cheeks. She had hated it but forced herself to take it in good part, laughing, for initiations are meant that way; harsh, even spiteful. In the past crossing the line had been an alibi for cruelties; unspeakable things were done to cabin boys. Scapegoating.

Now there was celebration, a fancy-dress Neptune, a Triton and sea monsters; a small band played on deck and the worst was a gentle ducking in the swimming pool. Pink and green drinks were handed out, with polka-dot parasols on the rim of each glass.

Only the seasons were tossed overboard.

She hadn't minded the heat of the tropics. She found she had stamina others lacked and was elated by her lessened need for sleep. She had had her hair cut shorter. Late at night, she learned the stars were different in the southern hemisphere. Here, showing a different face, the galaxy crowded closer. In the clamour of its nearness, dawns and sunsets jangled the sky.

The earth had been remapped for her. She had spanned it and could now look at it entire, as if from a distance. Its girth at the Equator surpassed two dozen thousand miles. The earth was, after all, something measurable. It was in the tropics that its Pacific waters were deepest, the deepest of all, deeper in places than Everest was high. Here, then, you could plumb the earth's core, if only by echo-sounding.

When she thought of the children now it was by seeing this infinite but measurable world through their eyes. What would enchant them most would bring them back to her.

Dolphins, flying fish, camels and giraffes, parrots in the trees on the Isthmus, an elephant swaying through a Bombay thoroughfare. Creatures they could only see in zoos, or never at all. And butterflies of every hue, from ice white to pitch.

The Journeyman's Vision of the Future

'I swear the sun lies sometimes beneath me, for I am dazzled by it when I look down. It is a notion, I know. The rays catch on the rocks and make a stony mirror, but I am high up there and, breathing so free, I conjure with my body's lightness.'

His features glow in the windowlight that slants across the room. Tilting his head back, lost in his own words, he sighs, and into this defenceless pause there breaks a squawk of laughter.

All along the table, whose sides are crowded with travellers, the laughter rises and falls, peaking in raucous bursts at the far end, where the greasy platters sit in a steep untidy pile. Amid this hooting and hilarity, an elbow knocks against them and one crashes to the floor.

André is shaken sober by the din. He remembers himself and sees he might have sounded foolish, seemed comical perhaps, with his short-necked, stubby figure and the start of a

paunch that is pushing at his belt. Quick-eyed now, he hesi-
tates; then, as if merely caught out in his own drollery, he
gives a sage little nod of surrender, touching an eyebrow with
the tip of a finger, shrugging his mouth in a smile. A smile
that seals his lips.

The titters dwindle, stop, but a quietness draws itself around
him, tight. Ignoring it as hard as he can, André assumes a
vacant stare, casting his attention out through the gaping door
of the inn: at the sheer mid-day blue of the sky, at the tall,
skinny trees which disdain to shade the road running past, at
a curly-haired child dragging a wooden bird on a leash – a boy
of an age with his youngest. He had thought to have spoken
quietly; another jug of wine and his tongue will run away
with him, headlong into trouble.

After a while, his stubborn, dreamy silence wins, and he is
left in peace, spared the banter and the nagging questions.

His fretting is not for what is stowed in his pack. Two
pamphlets against the clergy, read, and to be handed on to
others. This is paltry smuggling, though he still might pay for
it were they found, and just a day or two in prison would be
sore injury to a man like him. Too long at the press and he
feels caged, his body impatient with its rootedness, his
thoughts climbing and wandering high above the even, rhyth-
mic clatter of machines. He likes to come and go as he pleases.
No locks on his weeks and months, no bars between him and
the sky.

He can see the risk is trifling; he is nobody, too small a fish
for police spies to notice, when they are looking out for
whole wagonloads of books.

A small risk is like a bite of the mountain air he thrives on.

Because of it his face has taken on the colour of tobacco. His muscles have long since toughened and he is nimble, though slower now on the hard uphill paths. He knows the time will come before long when he has to seek work nearer home.

Unless.

His other secret. This one hidden for fear of fiercer mockery than he has tasted already.

Once, before they reached Besançon, half-drunk on the thyme-scented nectar that filled his lungs, his senses sharpened by the purity of altitude into a moment's grasp on nature's eternity, he thought he glimpsed the crystalline spaces other men would fill after him, and he talked of it. Of a time to come when artisans no longer need scale the Jura's slopes, when a journeyman might travel untramelled by weather and snaggy terrain, casting off the slowness of the ground, and soaring like a swift, speeding faster than a goshawk in pursuit of a jay.

'And the price of the journey, Monsieur André. The masters would be saved what the labour of our legs costs them. It's only our hands that they'd pay for then, André. Their gain, not ours it would be.'

Another, the youngest, the compositor, capped the merriment that followed: 'You're surely not so old for walking, Monsieur André, that you have need of wings?'

He is in his prime. Not yet forty. As a younger man, he would have judged the schemes he cherishes as simple-minded dreaming. But the young have less need of other powers than their own, and no foresight of their own frailty, of strength ebbing on a long road. He is not fearful, only a pinch wiser.

Work is not always where you wish to find it, and it has been his misfortune more than once in recent years that after payment of the journey and a month at the press he has been sent on his way again, chasing employment in the Neuchâtel printshops then half across France.

So now he will shed his blind trust in circumstance and plan carefully for recklessness.

There have been better days and he believes that they will surely come again. When the sun shines and the wages are paid it is a life to be envied. He has known fellowship and witnessed many small wonders on his travels: been to Paris, where in his lodgings was a black man nearly as tall as a lamp-post, and where once he saw a servant girl put in a trance and made to walk on hot embers; been to Rouen and watched all manner of things unloaded from ships – strange spiky fruits, monkeys staring out from wooden boxes . . . and everywhere he has followed word of new inventions.

He had a trade to take pride in, though pride can lead to fisticuffs and tavern brawls have broken out in towns and villages all along the road. Gentle-tempered as he is, he has given and taken his own share of knocks, and has a white puckered scar on his cheek to remember a certain Thuringian by. The man's dark angry eyes had at first made André mistake him for a southerner, and this had caused him rude offence – though André saw too late that little was needed for that. It seems to him that Frenchmen and Germans are well inclined to fight, and the Swiss too, who are to be found wherever you go. Even as far as Constantinople, they say.

How many miles has *he* walked since the day his apprenticeship ended? He can no more easily count them than he can reckon all the ems of type he has pressed on to paper. Ink from the *Encyclopédie* has stained his hands and its authors' names are well imprinted on his memory, with a legion of others and their books; writers of tracts, concocters of lubricious libels on the king and the nobles, for which these days there is much demand in France.

How many more miles will he walk?

Were it some day possible to travel thirty leagues in an hour with a fair wind blowing, as Abbé Desforges had calculated, and even twenty-four without it, he might easily travel to Neuchâtel and return the same evening home to Troyes in time for supper, a day's work done. Desforges failed with his hinged flying machine, but many since then have judged his attempts to be near success; that was 1772 and news of them is still in the *nouvelles*. They are written of, moreover, in scholarly books. For all André knows, the Abbé has perfected his invention by now.

Desforges heartens him, but Bolori is his spur. Bolori flew. And in André's own city of Troyes.

More than two centuries have passed since then.

Thinking of Bolori, the journeyman shifts inside his body and in imagination stands with his arms held out level and his fingers splayed in an imitation of wings. A leap from the great tall tower of Saint-Pierre et Saint-Paul, and, feathers flapping on their springs, then fanned wide and majestic, Bolori sweeps across the sky, gliding towards the early morning sun.

So the story goes. When he's up on the Jura peaks, his agile limbs filled with aerodynamic conviction, the element of air clothing him and promising to break the pull of gravity, André can easily believe it.

Instead of flying due east, they say, Bolori veered south-eastward, high over the thin blue ribbon of the Seine, following the very path that André, airborne, would take. Towards Langres, the native town of Monsieur Diderot, high-walled and protected on its hilltop.

It might well have been that Bolori's true destination was even further, perhaps beyond the mountains. For the mountains are there to be conquered by flight. Flight, André now believes, will end every boundary and barrier to man, giving free passage to all things forbidden by frontiers, the knowledge of books among them.

Bolori got no further than the priory at Foissy.

André pictures him falling, dizzy and surprised. And seeing, as he falls, a curious sight: a throng of figures garbed in black and white, propelled this way and that on the green meadow beneath him, seeming to roll like particoloured balls. The nuns must have been beside themselves with fear and won-derment as this fallen angel entered their midst. Women, thinks the journeyman, will never fly; their cumbersome, rounded bodies and flapping skirts will always weigh them down, condemning them as earthbound creatures, bereft of any hope of aerial release. How sad it must be to be born a woman, when even the lowest of men begin to cry out for their freedom.

Denis Bolori was a clockmaker, and André has even seen his handiwork on the clocktower at Rigny. Now there was a craftsman; the clock, it was said, kept good sun-dial time.

André thinks, with contempt, of the men who work in Japy's factory, their skills divided into parts, made shoddy by the master's mean trimming of their time. Working fast, yet still ill-paid. From Beaucourt they sometimes find their way to Besançon and in this very inn wine was spilt and blows were dealt against some four or five of them.

The watch movements they make will do only for the Swiss manufacturers, who are known to set store by cheapness and quantity. In other things too they will sell good men short; André has heard of how they let women work in the trade at Geneva, though in the rougher parts of it, and some to do the gilding with mercury. It saddens him to see so debased what was once a true artisan's job: setting the movement of time, fashioning it into an object both beautiful and accurate.

Be a hostage to time and you are bound forever. Men must make time their servant.

Having eaten and drunk well enough, and having had their fill of the rowdy tavern talk, André and his three journeyman-companions take to the road again, striking out for Langres, and soon leave Besançon rising behind them in the dust. They are in no great hurry to be home; wine-mellowed and doused in the heat of early summer, they set themselves an idle pace. Their slowness lulls the afternoon, lengthening the minutes and the hours into bliss that seems to stretch the skin of time forever. A fine June day in 1785, when the earth, though old, is still elementally young and unspoiled, little marked by the tearing explosions of progress. Four men walking north, languid under a cloudless sky.

In his mind's eye, André sees Bolori tilt into a shining vertical and a feather-tip scrapes the ground before the body's crash.

Now he strides along, feeling smooth against his palm the years-worn grain of his hazelwood stick, lifting his face to the sun as he walks. His eyes are half-closed. He listens to the song of a lark as it sails up from a nest in the meadow they are crossing. Around him a rust-coloured butterfly daubed with white teases ragged circles, then it suddenly skims clear away. Small flying things lap the fragrant air: birds, wasps, bees and dragonflies that softly hum and buzz and whirr, and with an ache of anticipation André's senses begin to inhabit this easeful, volant world.

In Neuchâtel he has talked to a man whom he can trust, a carpenter very versatile in his competence, so that making light-feathered wings which will move when André bids them to will prove no great difficulty. It is his plan to have them variously built, testing different curvatures for compression of the air beneath, or straightness so that they might cleave the air like oars, whether yielding with springs or with hinges, with cords or brass wire; and to have them fit in altering lengths and scale, so that he will accustom himself to each of them by practice, in time being able to bear the widest span and heaviest weight. For it is this, he believes, that is needed to carry him beyond what Desforges and Bolori achieved. For this he has more money saved than his wife could imagine. In September he goes back to Neuchâtel . . . provided things continue as they should, and he has for sure the work that has been half-promised.

It may take a year, perhaps two, or three. For now, dreaming of flight, and brushing the air with its certainty, the Journeyman is at one with the world.

★

Can you see him, in a lemon haze of early autumn sunlight, spinning up from the ridge of the Crêt de la Neige, or poised on that fatal edge of the Echelles de la Mort, then plunging? Maybe climbing in the air's fast stream and borne by it sublimely westward; making a truce at last with gravity? Or dipping in an instant's cruel surrender, a proud human angel denied its heaven?

Or perhaps now you can see him, closer, flailed by time, at last become a slave to speed; a fast-pinioned shadow on a wall.

Alida Valli's Coat

On the day the divorce was made final she received a red rose from the man who had been her husband. She opened the card that came with it: *For Stella. I wish you well, Ian*, and thought about the meaning of this message.

She suspected the rose, red and perfect as it was; the belatedly romantic gesture of an unromantic man. It was surely not his thought behind it, but the next wife's prompting. And the words were the thorn. As if he had all the wellness to wish and she had none. For, though she'd left him, one ordinary day walking free of a marriage that staggered after only two years, he was now partnered and she was alone. So this was his ending, not hers.

Stella looked at herself as they might see her, and found herself wanting. Her life had not been renewed as she'd hoped. The same children's faces looked back at her each morning in the classroom. She was becalmed in the routines of work and in singleness. Imperceptibly, her youth, the very thing she'd counted on in inviting freedom, was beginning to slip away. She was twenty-five, and this was what she thought as she looked at herself and the rose.

This ending urged change on her. A holiday would help; somewhere she'd never been. Alone. She would go at Easter, which was late that year. She'd been reading George Eliot's *Romola* and she thought at once of Italy.

But Stella feared disappointments. She mistrusted the known and the overly praised. Just as roses were suborned, so the beautiful places of the world could be robbed of their true splendours by the trade in tarnished images, all the meanings at their heart sucked out. Venice was now shrunk inside the plastic key ring the school secretary used for the stationery cupboard keys: a luminous bulge of gondola, lagoon and sky. The Colosseum covered one corner of a rayon headscarf worn by the tenant downstairs, and Pisa's leaning tower was all she knew of Pisa. As her finger toured the map it bypassed Florence altogether. She disdained the prior attractions that might blight discovery. Instead, at a friend's suggestion, she chose a small northern city where tourists seldom went. It had its share of architectural features and the food was reputed to be very good.

The friend had a brother studying there, and once the flight was confirmed, Alexander was asked to find Stella a hotel: 'A small, old-fashioned place, charming but comfortable', he wrote, having booked it. This was roughly what she'd asked for.

She had arranged things so that nothing would fail at least to match her expectations. Nor did it. Reaching the city at sunset, she found it at its most tantalising, poised between day and night. In the dusk its arcaded streets and spacious squares brimmed with yellow light. Their bustle charmed her at once, making her glad of the evening ahead, yet impatient for the fullness of the day. At the hotel, a note from Alexander asked her to meet him later at a nearby café; a neat little hand-drawn map showed her where.

Alexander too was small and neat. She wouldn't have found him if he hadn't called her name as she stood scanning the tables, looking for an English face and finding none. She was welcomed in a flurry of names and handshakes, amid the commotion and smiles of his friends. Her drink was ordered, her plans established, then claims on her were made. Silvia, Alex's girlfriend, would collect her next morning for a sight-seeing tour and they'd have lunch. Others proposed dinners and concerts, a drive to the coast. They talked non-stop, laughing and arguing, it seemed to Stella, about how they should entertain their guest. In the space of an hour she felt already changed by the sudden hospitality of these benign strangers. Their vivacity flowed into her. She looked at Alex, seeing a chameleon, Italian in his skin, transformed in the smallest of his un-English gestures, and wondered how easy it was.

It occurred to her that, just by staying here, she might become someone else altogether.

Into this gusty spring evening gaiety walked a man who had an air of good-humoured melancholy. Alex and the rest called out as he passed. He smiled but didn't stop. On the way back from the ice-cream counter, pistachio cone in hand, he was asked to join the gathering; he shook his head and made a sign that seemed to indicate impossibility. Then, changing his mind, he shrugged surrender, and pulled up a chair next to Stella. Stella was not given to smiling at strangers, but the smile she turned on him was the smile of a drowsy woman revived by the generosity of her new surroundings. It was the smile of euphoria and its spontaneity surprised her.

He did not stay long, but he was the one she remembered most as she lay awake, her insomnia buoyed by excitement and too much espresso. What she remembered was to do with the concentration in his eyes, their alert but inward look.

The city wasn't large; its centre, where the long arcaded streets converged in a scattering of squares, was compact. Its geography lent itself to chance encounters, so it wasn't strange that the following afternoon, wandering and gawping at the passing scene, she should meet Leone – for this was the name of the quiet, watchful man who'd sat next to her the night before. Not his real name; a nickname. He told her it meant 'lion', as they spoke in shaky French at the bar where she'd noticed him sitting and he'd waved her over.

It is artificial enough to speak in a language not your own and in which you're unpractised, but when neither participant in a conversation is at home with the words they exchange, these acquire an acute and self-conscious formality. When strangers wish to be intimate, but must observe certain social preliminaries, language is an awkward, resented intermediary: too slow, too false. Its banishment is longed for. Here, at least, its inadequacy was avowed, its provisional, partial power laughed off, and other kinds of speech allowed. Formality persisted, nonetheless, but the very effort of language that had to be made convinced them of a motive: desire perhaps.

This romance both was and wasn't. A courtship begun

with abrupt intensity in a cobbled square named after a composer of operas (not a very well-known one, though; Rossini and Verdi were a few streets away), it got no further than its dazzling overture. Leone kept a distance from the friends who had introduced them, but appeared at unexpected moments across Stella's path. In this mysteriousness, Stella – *une étoile tombée*, as Leone had called her; a star fallen across his path – found only added magic.

By day the air was soft and the sky serene blue, but by night with Leone everything hung suspended in a different element, a nocturnal density, like in a dream, or underwater, or like being leading actors in a film. They would walk arm in arm through the quiet streets, and drink *grappa*, either at his flat, a white-painted attic whose most prominent furnishings were an architect's drawing-board and high shelves of books, or in a bar called *Il Dado*, that was long and narrow and smoky. 'It reminds me of Prohibition,' he told her one night. 'We could be Hollywood gangsters in the thirties.' The time-warped atmosphere felt right to Stella, as if they had the past at their bidding, as well as present and future.

For they could have been anywhere, though the city itself was a part of the trance; and they could well have been in another time, so little attachment did they have to their own. It was one day short of a week from her arrival when Stella perceived another aspect of this timelessness; each time together was like the first: a brief, exciting collision, and then a parting full of desire for what was to come. The way fish dart and glide and barely touch, flashing silver.

Leone asked her to stay. She couldn't. Then he asked her to return, to travel with him to the ruins and volcanoes of the south, to return and stay forever. But he never embraced her with more than a tentative touch of love, and never seemed to want her as his lover. When, on the seventh night, she asked him why, he said that it would happen, he was only saying a long goodbye to someone else.

The next night she waited, but he didn't come. There was no answer when she phoned. At his flat the morning after, a man she had never seen before said he'd left the city for a day or two. Before setting out for the airport, she pushed a note through his door with her London address on it. She was desolate.

Desolation ended on her return to Kentish Town. Now, feeling herself to be transformed, she forgot desertion. Distance removed her from it, replacing loss with separation. 'I am in love,' she proclaimed, sleepless at night from the joy of it. Holidays are like that, their sorest instabilities salved by reality once we come back to it.

By day she thrived, despite the sleeplessness; the pallor she'd come back with instead of a suntan had a sheen to it, her hair gleamed, her eyes sparkled. She believed without doubt that Leone loved her.

She waited for a letter, for the phone to announce his voice with distant static, and even an unexpected ring at the door made her heart knock. She waited, with the tears drooping from her eyes as she put on the kettle first thing in the morning. At night she wept too, after asking herself what she could have done to provoke abandonment and cut love short. The summer evenings lengthened and in her loneliness she felt diminished as before; smaller, slower, like Alice rubbing her eyes after Wonderland. Winter came, an anaesthetic, and grey life settled round her once again. Christmas brought cards with pale Italian postage stamps, and when she saw that his was among them, curt and cordial like the rest, she had no more hope. Which was not to say that she forgot.

Stella ten years later was sure and self-possessed. Her life, far from dull, was busy with interests and pleasures. She had no children of her own, but for the children of others she devised new ways to make schooldays brighter and more fun. Still safe from education cuts, the teachers' centre where she worked was crammed with games and books and infantile audio-visual aids, software and micro-computers for the under-twelves. When she put her work away, there were friends and the man in her life: Tim, divorced, father of two little boys.

Tim still had family ties; he would even drop everything, including their weekend plans, attentive to his ex-wife's cries of crisis. Mumps, measles and Rose's faulty central-heating had all intervened. Stella minded when this happened; she hated being given no warning, but was otherwise happy enough that Tim's residence in her life was only semi-permanent.

Tim, a librarian who bore a resemblance to James Stewart, was a film buff, and Stella came to share this passion. She found that films entered daily life like memories, so that she was frequently being reminded of them, in faces and situations, in the way space and light created a mood of imminent drama, of normality waiting to be interrupted. A familiar film would draw you inside it and compel you with its details: the time on a clock, the pattern on a carpet, the way an actress's hat sat on her head, like Alida Valli's hat in *The Third Man*, which Tim had on video.

They had watched it often and by now Stella judged Harry Lime to be a spirit of intransigence, rather than evil. A Mephistopheles, a Don Juan, a larger figure than a thief; overseeing corruption, not just embodying it. Alida Valli was on his side, a beautiful woman without a home, no less uncompromising than her satanic, handsome lover. It seemed to Stella that Alida Valli's coat was a part of this pride. It swaggered as she moved, fluid and elegant, but it was also a coat for keeping out weather and loneliness, for facing Vienna's dark ruins and capricious Cold War bureaucrats; a generously cut New Look coat with a necessary severity in the collar and the solid shoulders. She wore it sometimes belted, sometimes not. It was the only possible coat for her stubborn exit in the film's closing scene, when she walked that tree-lined road, alone and at last no longer in the shadow. Stella began to scan the rails of second-hand shops and surplus stores with fifties stock, in the hope of finding another like it.

For Stella, Alida Valli existed only in that coat. Then, one night on BBC2, they showed *Senso*, and Stella videoed it. This time Alida Valli was the nineteenth-century countess Livia, sacrificing everything for passion in an operatically tragic story of love and betrayal that begins with an opera on stage in Venice. In both films she survives her lover's ignominious death, though here destruction of a different kind becomes her own fate.

After seeing the film, Stella remembered her trip to Italy. She had never been abroad since, except for a weekend in Paris with Tim. He liked to take the children with them in the summer and it was easier to stay in England. She watched *Senso* again and again, and a desire to return to Italy began to take hold of her. Not to the city she already knew, no, she would avoid too close an encounter with memory; but to Venice. Tim didn't want to leave the children, so she would go alone, just a week, at Easter.

She arrived in the evening. In the Grand Canal and the moss-hemmed palaces that rose out of it, where shadows and reflections rocked against water and stone, she recognised an aqueous universe where she might feel at home. This beauty, of night silence and tangy air, was unforeseen. It induced a sense of rapture.

In four days of wandering, eluding other tourists, and finding in the city's labyrinth secret corners that seemed wholly of the past, she lost herself. Venice possessed her. Everything in her London life was now remote and unreal, as if it, not her holiday, had been temporary. She surrendered to the present and its seductive peace. Her sense of renewal was absolute, something she had longed for unknowingly for years.

On the fifth day she found herself in a square in what had once been the Jewish Ghetto. The buildings here were very tall and tall plane trees vied with them in reach. She walked round the square to consider the view from every side. Then something struck her as familiar. She couldn't think what it was, but since she was carrying her camera she thought she would take a picture. Looking through the viewfinder, she realised. The building she had in her sights was known to her from *Senso*, in the very scene where Livia goes looking for her lover, Franz. How strange, she thought, here she was in the physical world of the film.

She approached the house. It must have been several

centuries old; grand on the exterior, it was now converted into half a dozen flats, she could see from the number of doorbells. One name caught her by surprise, for it was the same as Leone's. Two curious coincidences.

She went and sat for a while on a bench in the square, half-wondering whether the name's owner might indeed be Leone (although she could remember no connection of his with Venice). In the time that passed like this she saw an elderly woman enter the building and a boy with a dog come out. Should she or shouldn't she ring the bell? And then she saw him, a briefcase in one hand, in the other a net bag bursting with groceries; there was no mistaking this man making his way towards the door where Livia had sought out Franz. She intercepted him and held out her hand.

Leone's disbelief soon turned to delight. The telling of their stories began inside his bright kitchen once he had poured them each a glass of sparkling wine. In brief, he had married and divorced; his ex-wife lived in Rome with their son, and he lived alone. With the same succinctness, Stella unfolded her life and, finally, insouciant and pretending just to tease, she asked him why he'd ended their romance. He was perplexed at first, then, taking her hand and laughing in more genuine mockery, he told her it was *she* who had left *him*. He had never forgotten her. She knew that this was, logically, a lie, but also the truth.

That evening they had dinner together in a charming little restaurant unfrequented by tourists; the food was simple but delicious. A perfect meal. A perfect night. The moon shone brazen and numinous as they walked along a narrow quayside where the city reared up and turned its back on the lagoon.

There the boats at mooring creaked in the dark, their juddering sounds calling and answering, as if vessels denied the sea had a language for lament and longing.

Leone asked her to stay with him that night. Entranced, she agreed. Time had been erased and the promise of the past restored. She almost believed that whatever moment she'd chosen to penetrate the years between them, he would have been there, waiting.

All the same, when they reached his door she was tempted to pinch herself, suspecting a dream; which made her stop to consider this surrender to a phantom love affair. What might it mean for the future? All, or nothing? Did she belong here, or nowhere? Could she trust Leone, was he Franz or Harry Lime or just someone she had never really known? Doubt prevailed; it formed a grain of fear. Turning, she kissed him, then fled into the darkness, as he called her name after her, insistent and commanding. Impervious, she ran and ran.

This time she returned to London with relief at having regained home, and life began again. Some months later, she was rummaging through a second-hand clothes rail in the market near Tim's house, when she found a coat that seemed identical to Alida Valli's. Though the fabric was heavy, it fell from the hanger in soft and elegant folds. The label too assured her of its quality, the cut of its approximate date. It might well have been the very same coat.

Stella bought it, in great triumph, without even trying it on. She took it home and hung it in the wardrobe, where it stayed. Unworn.

The Untravelled World

The traffic is sporadic, but because it's the main coast road they cross holding the children's hands, sometimes all of them raggedly in a row: Miriam, little Liliana and her sister Loli, their mother, the *tata* and Juanito. On the other side, between the road and the beach, the rust-loaded tracks of a disused railway line depress the yellowing grass. In the first days, Miriam can't help but turn each time to face the ghost of an oncoming train. Another yard or two, and under the thin soles of her canvas shoes the ground loosens, sloping down.

July. The hot beat of late morning. It is always the same time when they walk across. They seldom see anyone else on the sand, even though there must be at least a dozen other bungalows along that stretch.

The *tata* has her dip, her dark freckled arms pumping in a sure line out to sea, further than the rest of them ever go. In less than fifteen minutes she is back, dressed, and gone to see to lunch and the unfinished chores.

Miriam swims with slow frog-like movements, playing with the two girls in the water. Their fearlessness makes her more and more at ease in the sea; that and the sea's own changelessness. The children's mother sits alone with three-year-old Juanito beside her in his sunhat. She surveys the shore, or reads a glossy picture paper purveying gossip about crowned heads and millionaires. If Miriam looks back she sees a lonely figure, incongruously upright in the collapsible chair beneath the straightly planted parasol, as if on a throne.

Close up, her regal solitude is a mirage. She is a boisterous, garrulous woman, her gaiety persistent, even when she pouts or frowns in annoyance at the children's naughtiness. She is never alone. Only, she swims very little, warding off the sun, for at thirty-two her neck is ruched and the skin around her eyes seamed with wrinkles. She makes a joke of her lined features, once telling Miriam that they bear the marks of suffering.

She grew up here in the south, and even in the parasol's shade her face tans; it is already the colour of cloudy tea, though not as brown as Miriam's.

After three weeks Miriam is browner than she has ever been. The transformation persuades her that further alterations may take place. She looks in the mirror more than she used to. She waits for things to happen to her body, as if she were still an adolescent.

Perhaps it is a condition of this that everything else should stay the same. She wakes each morning to a hot clear sky. On her walk to the bungalow, on the empty road busy with the scents of overburdened gardens, the sun's blaze, the sea's sparkle lock her in the spell of a perfect summer monotony.

Nothing disturbs it, but day after day the temperature is inching up, intensifying it, boring it into her.

Breakfast starts her day with the family: a bowl of coffee, thin toast imprinted with the stripes of the grill pan, and spread thick with butter and jam. Miriam is surprised at how new such familiar things can taste, their flavours and smells recalling nothing of Manchester and home.

Between ten thirty and eleven fifteen she gives the girls their first lesson. At their age learning needs to be play; she draws pictures for them and they tell her the names of things in English or ask her questions. As they talk she will add more objects or people. Her drawings are simple, hardly less crude than the ones the children do for her when the game is reversed.

Draw me an apple on a tree. Draw me a man going for a walk with his dog. Then, 'What colour is the dog? 'Is it a big dog?' 'Make the man's shirt blue.' 'Draw me his daughter coming to meet him.'

With each of the drawings they make up little stories, give the people names, describe the inside of the house that on paper consists only of a square-roofed façade with a door and the symmetry of windows.

The two sisters are not alike. Eleven-year-old Liliana, who has delicate features and neat plaits the same dull corn colour as Miriam's hair, will be a fearsome beauty, as her mother must have been in the bloom of her youth. She is imperious, bent on showing Loli the advantage of her years. And yet protective too. Loli, who is eight, is soulful and sweet-faced, prone to tears. Her plumpness, her unruly chestnut hair and thick eyebrows promise none of her sister's premature elegance. She has become attached to Miriam, and Miriam is touched by her affection, and entertained by Liliana's lively cunning.

Like their mother, they call her 'Mees Meeriam'.

Miriam is uneasy with the household's unequal currency of names. The *tata* addresses her as *señorita*. She does not use this in return; it seems too singular, all the other adults call her Concha. Miriam avoids names as much as she can.

The *tata* serves them at table under the pergola, then eats alone in the kitchen. She is perhaps the children's mother's age, but handsome and more vigorous, with a pinned-up bush of apricot hair. Miriam's guilt towards her is tinged with awe.

The arrangement requires Miriam to give the children English 'conversation' and lasts until four in the afternoon, when they have the *merienda*. She isn't expected to insist too much, just to foster certain habits of speech. To wear certain words and phrases into prompt daily use. 'Pass me the bread, Liliana, please.' 'Loli, do you like this salad?'

On the beach, the easy sibilance of sand and sun, sea, shells and swimming is rehearsed every day. Yet the words are not always remembered, and their ritual overuse provokes the children's laughter.

In her room at the *pensión* Miriam is sometimes jerked into wakefulness by the wheezy braying of a donkey. At first she failed to recognise the sound. Once she attaches it to the animal she sees in the shed next door she begins to wonder at the cause of its distress. Hunger or pain? As time goes on these noises seem closer to her window, intruding more and more on her early morning sleep.

The village has two kinds of inhabitants: those who live in the low whitewashed houses all year round, have sun-scorched hands and faces and wear cheap, badly-fitting clothes. The others come only in the summer months, and in Holy Week. Mothers with their children open up the winter-shuttered bungalows and apartments, for the summer is long and the fathers come from the cities only in relays.

Tucked at the bottom of one of the apartment blocks is a café, with a jukebox and white moulded plastic chairs and tables. Miriam goes there in the evenings, since there's nowhere else. Only a bar, where women never go. Miriam doesn't need anyone to tell her this.

One night in the café she meets Raúl. His father, a haulage contractor in the city a dozen miles along the coast, owns one of the apartments four floors above. Raúl is there with his mother, his brother and three sisters. He is twenty, and the oldest son.

He becomes the companion of Miriam's evenings, which until then have been solitary. Sometimes, late in the evening, she has walked along the beach road and seen a light in the pergola behind the children's bungalow, and heard voices crack against the heavy night air, and she has pictured the children's mother and their grandparents from the bungalow next door; but just in the way she might imagine the movements of any disembodied strangers on the far side of a darkened garden fence. Because she is glad to be out there, invisible and free of her connection to them.

When Raúl walks with her on the beach, he takes her hand. There are evenings when they drive along the coast and drink icy *cuba libres* on a terrace overlooking the sea, and he gives her little furtive kisses. At ten he goes home to have supper with his family.

A high white wall with a door set in it turns out to be the frontage of the village cinema, open only on Saturdays. They go to the first midnight showing; the film is a comedy called *How to Murder Your Wife*. There is so much laughter and loud shouting at the screen that Miriam misses at least half of the dialogue and she cannot see what is funny. As they make their way to the exit, the spat-out shells of sunflower seeds lie thick around their feet. Outside, Miriam sees that the audience, many of them still laughing, now fills the village street, so that it appears overrun with the remnants of some carnival or orgy. It is 2 a.m.

On Saturday nights to come, waves of sound, mingling live human uproar with amplified music and speech and gunfire and screeching brakes or horses' hooves will crash against the interior walls of the roofless building and spill over them, breaking into her sleep or her concentration on a book.

Raúl is torn, he confesses. He would like to be her lover, but he is not in love with her. He lives by too many rules and ambitions for rashness to intervene; imagined consequences waylay him. His heroes are his father, who rose from poverty to prosperity through hard work and a decisive character; and Aristotle Onassis, whose millions were the product, Raúl believes, of sheer self-discipline. Raúl is a student of economics. He reads the biographies of famous men.

Raúl is kind and his mild good looks reassure her, but she is not in love with him either. She refuses him the encouragement she thinks is all he needs to make him change his mind. She would like something more than this half-heartedness. At home there is a boyfriend, a relic of her schooldays, who is spending the summer working in a brewery. She sends Andy postcards with pictures of palm trees and bougainvillaea.

Miriam's room is poor and bare in a way that doesn't matter in the south; she is glad of its cheapness. But two things begin to bother her. There are no shutters and when she leaves in the morning she pulls the window open and closes the thin curtains against the sun. In the afternoons she returns to find the room invaded by wasps, two, three or sometimes four of them, purposeful in the shade and unwilling to be banished. When their numbers increase she becomes aware of the nest, just outside the window.

The man who owns the *pensión*, whose teeth are rotten and whose name is Señor Andrés, is sympathetic about the wasps. He reaches out and, with the blade of a long knife, knocks the nest away.

It is when she goes to him one night about the lizards that he laughs at her. She anticipates this, nervous, remembering how, as a child, she would wake her father if she found a cranefly or even an extra-large moth in her room late at night. Her father, who rose at six for work, would be angry. She cannot help her fear of the lizards. The children say they spit, their grandfather tells them this; *salamanquesas* spit acid that burns the skin. Often when she switches on the light she sees them streak across a wall and through the open window. But one night she is in bed, a book in her hand, and her gaze strays upwards. Two parallel green lines lie flat on the ceiling, eyes staring down at her, and she thinks they could drop on her face. Outside, in the black whirr of midnight, in her broderie-anglaise-edged pink nightdress and matching cotton housecoat, she stands at the door where Señor Andrés frowns, rubs sleep from his eyes, and goes to fetch a broom. He brings a cat for good measure. Afterwards the cat's mouth is a mess of blood and scaly green. It disgusts her.

The second time this happens Señor Andrés waves her away at the door, his face creased in annoyance. She insists that the lizards spit. He tells her they're harmless. '*No le hacen nada.*' He climbs the stairs, exasperated. He repels her; she hates to have him in her room. She also suspects he is right.

The children's father arrives from Madrid, a dark, thickset man, saturnine and handsome. He wears khaki shorts, and the curling black hairs that cover his legs and fur his thighs re-emerge at the open neck of his polo shirt. He is a lawyer. On the beach he reads works of Catholic philosophy.

After her husband's arrival, the children's mother begins to talk to Miriam about the family, as if his presence has broken the August somnolence that stifled thoughts of life elsewhere. Her father-in-law, a man she never knew, hid for two years from the Reds in cellars and sewers, eating potato skins and whatever refuse he could find.

'*Los Rojos*'.

Miriam sees that her eyes and lips stiffen on the words.

She confides to Miriam that her husband is most passion-ate in the afternoons; in the long siesta after lunch when the children are having their second English lesson.

This intimacy unsettles Miriam, since she cannot return it with something of her own, and she knows she is not expected to.

★

One night she sees the wasps have returned. They have rebuilt their nest in the same place as before. It needs to be burned so as to destroy all traces. Señor Andrés reproves her, as if she should have known. In the morning sunlight, pale flames consume the cells, leaving a scorch mark on the wall.

At lunch Miriam notices how the children's father changes things. His wife is still boisterous, leading the children's laughter, but their grandparents seem subdued. Grandfather no longer tells the off-colour jokes that prompt his daughter's cries of '*viejo verde*'. Grandmother, whose loud chatter often rises to the level of a shout, now lowers her voice for her son-in-law's ears. Yet he seems oblivious, as if they could never perturb him. He smiles a quiet indulgent smile; perhaps vulgarity mattered little in the bargain he struck with his marriage to a woman of such sensual animation. And it occurs to Miriam that this may not be vulgarity at all, just the buoyant temperament of the south.

It was on a visit to the south, Miriam learns from the children's mother, that her husband happened to see her and fell in love with her when she was only a schoolgirl of seventeen. He discovered where she lived and went to her parents to make himself known. They married two years later. Miriam finds this story unappealing, though as a fairy-tale it might have charmed her; a fairy-tale with some ambiguity at its centre. But it is true.

The angel of purity the man sought out, the smooth schoolgirl beauty has been erased altogether from this woman's ravaged face. It seems like a face whose future only dates from now, not from fifteen years earlier, a face grown into, out of blankness. It has no past, no imprint of that bridal profile

Miriam has glimpsed in a silver frame. Miriam thinks of her mother's face, wearing middle age like an ill-fitting mask; the wrinkles, the sag-lines, the bags under her eyes appearing traced or stuck on, the way actresses in family sagas are made to age. Its former prettiness is flagrant, nostalgically proclaimed.

The children's mother confides in her again. About the nightmare of three childbirths, the last of which endangered her life. This, from such a strong, broad-hipped woman, surprises Miriam.

'I won't have any more.' She shakes her head for emphasis, clenching her lips. Miriam doesn't ask whether this is a decision or an outcome. Whether the mouth is bitter or only rueful.

Miriam arrives for breakfast one morning to find that the two girls have had bad insect bites as they slept, Loli on her arm, Liliana on an eyelid that is now dramatically swollen. Not mosquito bites, their father is sure, some kind of spider perhaps, mildly poisonous.

That afternoon, Miriam is standing under the pergola, half-leaning against the kitchen wall, when Loli shrieks, and directs a shaking finger to a spot behind her.

The spider must measure at least eight inches in diameter; it is white-legged, with a mauve body that shades to pink. At a safe, shocked distance Miriam finds it beautiful. The grandparents agree that this can't have been the one that bit the girls. No one touches it. Then the *tata* lifts the paperback book Miriam had been reading after lunch and strikes out at the insect. It falls to the ground, a tangled ball of coarse white threads.

★

Each week earns Miriam a day of freedom. She takes the red bus along the coast to the city, sinking back in the seat to raise the bare backs of her lower thighs away from the burning plastic upholstery. Twice she has been driven there by Raúl, when her day coincided with an errand his father had for him. But she doesn't mind going alone; she needs no one with her to enjoy the city, provincial town though it is, and always has hopes that some adventure will befall her. She window-shops, has lunch in a seafood bar, and later in the afternoon eats an ice-cream at one of the busier café terraces, where she can watch people go by, stepping to the right and left of the jasmine sellers. When someone does stop to buy from one of them, she wishes it were for her.

Her hair has grown long and thick in the sun, and on one of these trips to the city she decides to have it cut. Cropped, it comes in feather-points to the lobes of her ears. Now nothing will be slapping at her neck as she swims, and her face will be free when she dips underwater. She'll feel all the more a part of her new element.

It is soon after, among the crowd of the evening *paseo*, that she is stricken.

Her right arm feels stiff, aching dully and suddenly weak. As she continues to walk through the centre of the city, supporting this arm with her left hand, she feels the pain get worse. On the bus back her head begins to throb and by the time she's in the village she can hardly see.

In the course of the night clear words like sunstroke don't form in her mind. She just lies with her head exploding and time smashed into the atoms of delirium, hanging on till morning.

After Señor Andrés has telephoned, the children's mother comes, around eleven, with headache pills and fruit juice. 'You have to remember, ours is an African sun.' She sounds boastful. In the mid–August days, the sun's ferocity has peaked. Miriam catches up on sleep, then goes out to buy a cotton cap.

Raúl tells her how dangerous the sunstroke could have been and she is grateful for her ignorance. He has been reading a biography of Einstein. As they walk that evening through the village street and down the narrow avenue of trees which take them to the beach, he begins to explain the theory of relativity. Miriam has never heard of it before and fails to grasp the sense of it. Raúl is happy to explain it all again.

As August ends, the children's father leaves to attend to his clients, and their mother spends more time in the bungalow next door with her parents.

Miriam doesn't see Raúl every day. Now and then, he disappears into the city, leaving a larger gap than usual between their meetings. When this happens Miriam feels exposed to a forgotten loneliness that she hadn't known existed before Raúl, except perhaps as anxiety. Yet even if he doesn't come back he will have been what was necessary: she couldn't have gone home without there having been 'someone she'd met'. She knows he thinks he means more to her than he does and this vanity of his gives her secret satisfaction; for someone as serious as Raúl, vanity ranks as stupidity.

At the café on one of these evenings when she is alone, sitting outside to escape the noise of the pinball machine, she notices two men whose faces are unfamiliar. After a while she realises she is being stared at, and turns to look at them.

It is the younger of the two, a man of around thirty she thinks, who has his eyes on her. He smiles; not a warm quick smile meant to charm, but a smile seeming only to confirm his stare, to take it a stage further.

He asks if she is French. She takes this as a compliment, laughs, shakes her head. Being English is maybe not the worst thing in the world, but here she is always reluctant to admit to it. When she does, he nods, slowly, as if to say he ought to have known. His companion shows no interest in these conversational gambits, only drawing on his cigarette as if it required all his concentration.

Her new acquaintance is from Costa Rica. Miriam has only a hazy notion of where that is. Somewhere in South America?

He asks if he can buy her a beer. When she accepts, after a whispered exchange with his companion, he comes over to her table and sits with her. He is a journalist. He writes about sport: football and bullfights. He reminds her of a bull, with his prominent light blue eyes set in a square, strong-boned face and light hair that curls close to his scalp; face and head are sculpted as a unity. They wear a look of outraged boredom, of contempt for where he is.

He isn't easy or likeable. He is quite different from Raúl or the friends of his she has met. Like her, he has no real attachments here, he is privileged to be passing through. This is what attracts her to him and why she agrees to meet him the following evening, to go for a drive.

In the car he says nothing. They speed west along the coast

as if towards a destination where talk will begin. But in the bright, noisy resort where they stop for a drink, they say little and don't linger, then the Costa Rican turns his car back the way they came. Of course he wants to go to her room with her. When she says no, they go to the beach instead, to the empty stretch between the village and where the line of bungalows begins.

It is a moonless night. Lying on the sand in this man's arms, which feel excitingly strange to her, and unsafe, she listens for the sea. It is silent, as stilled and as dark as the land, meeting it so closely you would know you had reached the water only when you felt it on your toes.

She pushes the Costa Rican away, disappointed with his undisguised impatience when he reaches for different parts of her body as if she wasn't there. He gets up, saying nothing, his shrug outlined in the darkness, his features too fogged to show her an expression.

She prefers to walk rather than get back into his car. It is only a little way.

The next evening there is no sign of him or his car or his companion, and she knows they have gone for good. She has a spasm of regret. He had treated her refusal as if it made her less of a woman, as if she were only a girl, perhaps a virgin, needing assurances. She thinks of how they might be different from her, these women of the kind he had expected her to be.

With September the summer seems to enter eternity. Hot as ever, it obliterates all memory of rain. Miriam has lost any sense of this as a season.

The girls are bored, bored with their English lessons, bored with the beach. One morning Miriam arrives to find they have captured a mole, imprisoning it in a shoebox. Later that week they have tied a large cricket to the base of the swing at the back of the garden. They are nervous of it, of the long saw-like leg their grandfather warns them is dangerous, liable to snap and tear at skin. Miriam wonders was he the one to catch the creature.

Soon the prisoners are released. The girls turn their attention to their little brother, chasing him, tickling him, cuddling him more than ever before; a squirming boy-doll.

They still follow the day's routine, its stale sequence of lessons and beach and meals. Miriam wants to see how deeply brown her skin can go, now that there's so little sun-time left. How much darker can she be than her original self?

One morning in the sea Miriam feels something viscous brush against her leg. Swimming becomes impossible. A plague of jellyfish invading the water that was once so limpid and benign. It happens nearly always at this time of year, the children's grandmother reminds them. Years before, someone had died from a sting, not a jellyfish of course, a Portuguese-man-of-war it must have been. A young woman.

In the last week of September it rains, after over three dry months. Stopping to catch the first drops on the backs of her outstretched arms, Miriam feels festive. To be so glad of rain is exotic. She sends a postcard to Andy to tell him so.

At the month's end, the family leaves. Miriam's agreed time with them is over. She says her goodbyes at the bungalow, handshakes for the adults, hugs for the children. Loli is in tears.

In the melancholy afternoon of that same day she goes

with Raúl to the city. Soon she will be home, where everything is different; home to the scudding autumn downpours,
to the china cats on her mother's mantelpiece, to a new university term, the first of her final year, and to Andy, who will
maybe have met someone else. Along with the gifts she will
take she will carry a store of new things that have happened to
her during this, her first summer abroad. She is looking forward to the memories she will share. For now, she and Raúl
are to pretend they are lovers sad at parting.

She makes love with him, for the first time. Before, she
sees the ending of a tension that has slackened as the weeks
have passed. Afterwards there's lassitude, the luxuriance of
lying in the secret pit of an afternoon that will never be
repeated.

Raúl had planned everything: the flat, barely lived in,
which he has borrowed; the small cassette player with tapes of
classical and flamenco guitar; the bottle of fizzy wine. She
finds the flat squalid, its atmosphere too starkly one of dereliction. Yet that squalor gives a glamorous edge to how she
thinks she will remember it.

Next morning she leaves on a trip that will fill the five days
between now and the date on her plane ticket. Raúl collects
her and her luggage and drives her to the bus station. When
she returns to catch her flight home, he will be travelling on
business with his father. They have exchanged addresses which
Miriam suspects they will never use; he gives her a collection
of poems as a present and she remembers seeing the book on
the table next to the bed they had shared the day before.

The bus climbs into the mountains, up where gaping villages

appear as if suspended, only existing to wait for passing traffic: rattling buses like this one; trucks hurtling heedless through the narrow corridor of rocks and buildings; cars shuttling north or south, between seasons. Dogs uncoil themselves from doorways to stand and bark at them, asking to be noticed.

Midway they stop. It is windy. Packages and sacks lean against the café wall, ready for loading, while the passengers drink weak coffee out of glasses. The café sells plastic bags of biscuits in twisted shapes and Miriam learns that these are local specialities. She buys one, but the biscuits taste old and she sees the bag has tiny holes in it.

Arrival disappoints. No palaces and fountains yet. Out past the bus station stretches a wide dusty road lined with warehouse buildings and petrol stations. She can see no taxis and it looks like a long way to anywhere.

She does a foolish thing. By the exit where the buses set down their passengers two men wait to tout rooms for tourists. There is no one but Miriam. When the older of the two, a sad-eyed limping fellow, points to a flat across the road, she gives in to tiredness and the lateness of the hour.

When she has taken the room and it dawns on her that she's there alone with this stranger, a faint anxiety begins to nag her. She sleeps fitfully, having propped a chair against the flimsy door. In the morning there is no sign of disturbance; she has been left in peace. She knows, after all, that she is invulnerable, for if innocence is dangerous it is also talismanic.

Walking, she discovers that the centre of the city isn't far. She finds a hotel and goes back for her luggage. The man shows no surprise and Miriam supposes that he is used to such hasty departures.

The city lives up to its fabled name, once she has passed the dingy outskirts and the dull façades of the lower town. Domes and arches, colour-fractured light on marble, water that rises to pattern the arabesques of stone and flow downhill in soft cascades.

After two days these riches become excessive, burdensome, their beauty too impenetrably perfect, and she looks for relief to the high peaks of the sierra. On her third morning she sets out early for the terminus of the little train that will take her there. The chill in the air warns her to wear a sweater, a thick one; she thinks of cold ahead on exposed mountainsides.

As the train moves steeply upwards on to a ridge, the watery sunlight brightens, hardening against the window-panes. They are high now, travelling level, on the first flat summit of wooded slopes, and Miriam has a sense of gliding among treetops. At each of the halts a village pokes out among the trees. Another ridge rises across a deep gully, but the real sierra is higher still and the snow is far away.

At the end of the line no village appears. Miriam gets off the train and finds a path continuing along the ridge. She begins walking.

She hadn't reckoned with the heat. Up here, from mid-morning to late afternoon, it is still summer. Walking, she begins to feel sticky and uncomfortable in her heavy sweater. She takes it off, tying it around her waist. Underneath she wears a skinny-strapped suntop that leaves her midriff bare.

First, a man comes swaying towards her astride a mule. As he gets closer she greets him. '*Buenos días.*'

Passing her, he answers, to her surprise, with words she though belonged only in westerns. '*Vaya con Dios.*'

Some time later, an elderly woman sitting side-saddle on a mule comes abreast of her, heading in her direction. Miriam greets her and asks if there's a village that way. The woman smiles broadly and says yes. She points straight ahead, as if mimicking Miriam's own gesture. Moving off, she turns and nods. '*Vaya con Dios.*'

Ten or fifteen minutes later, Miriam encounters her again. She has dismounted and is packing something into one of the paniers slung across the mule's back. Nearer, Miriam sees they contain green fruit.

The woman turns and smiles again. She raises a hand towards the trees beside them. Miriam now sees they are laden with figs. She smiles back at the woman, her gaze becoming more direct. She takes in the dark face cross-hatched with wrinkles, the several layers of ancient-looking garments swaddling her chest and shoulders: the long full skirt, the woollen sleeve that has started to unravel at the cuff.

Miriam strolls on, a little more slowly than before. In a matter of minutes the woman catches up with her. She is now astride the mule. She slows the animal's pace and they share the width of the path. They say nothing.

'Look!'

The woman's voice is a loud slap in Miriam's ear, much louder than it needs to be. 'Look!' she says again, and reaching over her head into a fig tree, she plucks out a fruit and hands it to her. 'Eat!' she says, with a headjerk of encouragement, and Miriam, hesitant but knowing she must accept the woman's gift, peels back the thick green skin of the fig and bites into its sweet pulp, a jewel-seeded redness whose extravagance is alarming.

They continue along the path for another half-hour, meeting no one. The village stays hidden out of sight until, abruptly, the line of trees ends and a clearing appears. Facing her are not the squat huddled village houses Miriam expects, but a long building two or three storeys high, of reddish stone and all the more imposing for its position on a slope. Another, identical building stands at right angles to this one. From every window hang streamers of red peppers drying in the sun.

She has been staring with such perplexity that she has failed to see the throng of children. But they have all seen her. As she advances up the little slope alongside the old woman, now leading her mule, the children gather towards her and with a shock that almost makes her jump, she perceives hostility in their faces. Behind the children are women, old and young, at windows and in doorways, watching silently. Among the children she notices some older girls and boys; teenagers not much younger than herself, their faces appear fiercest of all.

Eyes devouring this scene, Miriam can make no sense of it. She has spoken to no one, touched nothing, surely given no cause for offence. She can see, though, that these people are poor, with none of the modernised poverty she has come to take for granted on the coast. This place is truly distant from what she knows.

All of a sudden she begins to locate this acute sense of strangeness and difference as something in herself, rather than in the people now around her. She sees herself as they must see her. Is it this difference, so unthinkingly flaunted, that has become the object of their mockery. Her sun-bleached hair, her carefully made suntan, her tight beige jeans and her flesh-baring yellow suntop. 'Where are you going?' shouts one of the girls. 'To the beach?'

There is laughter. Then she hears the word repeated in the crowd. '*La playa . . . la playa . . . la playa.*' It becomes a chant, and one giggling child jabs a finger at the exposed flat skin of her stomach.

She turns to her elderly companion; from her she catches not a flicker of sympathy, nor of disapproval. She thinks she sees the hint of a shrug, perhaps the ghost of a smile, and she wonders whether there is something more to this hostility than her alien looks.

Then Miriam feels irritation. Is she to be driven out, for nothing, to swallow her hunger and forget the thirst the walk has given her? She asks the woman if there is somewhere, a bar maybe, where she can get something to drink, even just a glass of water.

The woman beckons her to come the other way, and they proceed, turning their backs on the children, along a little path that diverges, forming a V with the track that had been their approach. Just beyond this corner is a low building, dirt scummed over its whitewash. Male voices drift from inside it. A face peers out at the grimy window, which is too small to let her see past it. The woman enters but signs to her to wait outside.

Miriam looks back at the children, and at that moment one of them lifts a stone and hurls it towards her. It falls short. Another lands beside her. A third grazes her hip. She can see other arms raised. Throughout this assault she hasn't moved an inch.

The woman reappears, a glass of water in her hand, and the stones cease. Miriam is trembling.

'Drink,' the woman says, as if it were a command she might not obey, and she gives a smile Miriam can only be hopeful of, but cannot trust.

And she drinks, with many eyes upon her. Tilting it, she drains every drop of water from the glass, then hands it back.

She tells the woman she should go now; in spite of herself, the words have the tenor of a plea. The woman walks with her again, towards the children, towards the bend where the path back to safety begins.

They call out, they push around her, and they laugh. What am I, wonders Miriam, an intruder on some special day, or an unwelcome envoy from a future they've already glimpsed? A thief, as tourists are?

But no one lifts another stone.

Miriam, left at the edge of the village, sets out along the mule-track; never once looking back, and trying very hard to expel the taste of fear.

Undue Haste

When he rolls up the blind there are blisters of rain on the window-pane. While he's waiting for the water to boil he turns on the radio and the forecast says downpours, with the likelihood of flooding. Summer's ending is abrupt, over-subservient to the calendar. He thinks of the Labor Day weekenders heading up to the Falls and how they'll be disappointed. After he finds his lighter, sunk in his dressing-gown pocket, it won't work, so he dips a dead match in the cooker's gas flame.

The downstairs apartment's dog is sitting on the back steps. They leave it outside most days; sometimes it's still there when he gets in from work. It looks up at Tom and gives a perfunctory bark, then drops its head in a pose of dejection. The rain hugs its fur, which looks shorter, darker. He feels sorry for the dog. But he has never made friends with it; he doesn't want them asking him to feed it, or it getting attached to him.

In the grey light the kitchen depresses him. The patchy dark green walls, the split wood of the draining board – where he'd left some tuna in an opened can last night – the sixty-watt gloom, all depress him, like a scene from a life he has left behind. He should have gone by now, by today of all days. He remembers there are loose ends to be tied up first.

The cigarette steadies him, and the tea. He has lain awake for hours, hoping to get some more sleep before the alarm. When he woke he switched on the light to see the time and his first thought was that Jean would have just taken off. He wonders where the plane is now. Over Greenland, or nearly. She'll be looking forward to sunshine, picnics by the lake, all the things he wrote telling her about in the spring. For a few moments he buries his face in his hands, letting tiredness numb him.

People get the wrong impression about the weather here. They think of log cabins in midsummer heat with midges clouding the night air by the lakeside; fish leaping in the dark. They picture snug sleigh rides at Christmas, like in old black and white films. He hadn't bargained for the long Montreal winter, trudging in the snow from one employment agency to another. He was ill-clad and the wind bit at his ears and face. It stung his eyelids and pushed his breath back into him through raw nostrils and cracked lips. People called this twelve below and weren't shocked by it. They warded off the atrocities committed by the climate with central heating, fur coats and fleecy boots, hats with earflaps. He had money for none of it; his savings were being drained by the bare necessities.

He had been counting on Andy Curran to make things easier. Andy had been there a year and had written full of promises. Tom found him about to get married – to a French-Canadian girl. He'd thought he'd be staying with Andy, but after the wedding they moved out to the suburbs, and Josiane put her foot down about starting married life with a house guest. Sometimes she spoke to Andy in French when he was there, though he knew her English was fine. Once the baby came, he even felt awkward about going round at all. Andy fixed him up with a temporary job at the start. Two weeks, then nothing for a while. He told him to do more computer training if he wanted decent money. There were plenty of loading jobs going at the factory where his brother-in-law was a foreman, but Tom's game leg ruled that out as a stop-gap.

Montreal was a mistake. At Easter, hearing from a cousin who had come over on a college placement, he went down to Toronto to see how the land lay. He got a job right away. The Good Life came closer; here, he could almost see himself as Canadian. His letters to Jean were extravagant with optimism. He wrote often. He had been lonely for so long.

Now he needs to feel fresh, clean, more alive than his sleeplessness will allow. The needles of water on his back massage the tension out of his skin, but the flow gets too hot, it stabs at him too sharply, the shower-head needs replacing. He alters its angle, lets the water skim round him, and it builds a comforting cloud of steam.

When he shaves he nicks his chin in two places. He pats at the blood with the edge of the damp bath towel. Change happens to everyone, he reflects, his hand trembling a little, his memory adjusting to the present. Andy had changed, not just with marriage, but before that. The Andy he'd met when he arrived in Montreal was already different, as if looking over his shoulder all the time to see how things were working out. He even seemed smaller, his gangly frame striving to take up less space than it used to. And this was a big country.

There had been four of them: Tom and Andy, Jim Colvin and Phil Reid. The other three had looked out for him ever since school. He was always one of the boys without really being like them. He might lack their bravado, their physical quickness, their malice-tainted confidence with girls; it didn't matter, he was the outlet for their kindness. It came to seem in excess of what his limp, his orphaned childhood demanded. At twenty, he'd wondered when it was he'd signed the contract that led to the expectations he fulfilled. Nice Tom, rewarding the kindness he's given, careful to hurt nobody's feelings. Nice-looking too, fair-haired, open-faced, but able only to watch the way Andy could challenge a girl's eyes; could turn morose, and the girls would find his sullenness exciting, fancy they could cure him of it. They confessed these things to Tom, sometimes on what he'd considered dates. He betrayed the girls' secrets, of course, judging their trust a form of contempt. What he knew was relayed without emphasis, as befitted a diplomat. Jean didn't know any of that crowd when he met her.

He has no umbrella so he turns up his collar and makes a dash for it, ducking in and out of doorways. Sal's Café is just on the other side of the block, but by the time he reaches it there's a fringe of wet hair plastered to his forehead. 'You could use a coffee, I bet,' drawls Sally, giving him a sideways wink. He suspects sometimes Sally drawls for his benefit, in a kind of

mocking response to his own accent. There was something
funny about hers, anyhow. Could it be she's trying to mimic
him, doing it badly. He hasn't thought of this before, but is at
once reassured by her smile. Sally likes him.

He has a bigger breakfast than usual since he's late today.
Ham and eggs, pancakes and syrup, orange juice. He smokes
and feels much better now. The day no longer intimidates
him.

Jean was his first love. He'd glimpsed something of himself in
her, although she wasn't quite an orphan; her father had
walked out. When he remarried, her mother didn't want to
be an onlooker, so she moved with her daughter to where
they weren't known. They lived above a dry-cleaner's next to
the shoe shop where Esther was the manageress; refugees
from Renfrew in a place where 'incomers' stayed that way
after twenty-odd years.

Mother and daughter had the same wiry alertness about
them, an air of muscular determination. Jean swam well.
There were dark hairs on her forearms and a shadow over her
upper lip that excited him. Esther had kept her looks. She
plucked her eyebrows and wore shoes in the house, medium-
heeled, well polished. His aunt had always insisted on slippers;
for the sake of the carpets.

Jean's interest was tepid for a while, but all the time he pursued her, Esther made him welcome. He would drop round
there, and if Jean wasn't in, he would pour out his heart to her
mother. She was on his side. No question.

Jean was different after he'd been away, so his year in
London paid off in the end, though he came back jobless.

There had been somebody else, but she'd got over it. It had helped her make her mind up about him. 'I took you for granted before.' When she said this he saw she relied on him. It was a new feeling.

It's funny to think he would be married to her now if she'd said yes there and then. No rushing into things for Jean. Canada had appealed to her, though.

On the bus to the air terminal he wonders if he still loves Jean. He knows he stopped missing her soon after he met Duna. That was in May, while he was waiting for Jean's answer, and still lonely. It has stopped raining, but the bus splashes passers-by from the gutter troughs. He watches people shrink back from the kerb; a woman makes a little skip to dodge the dirty water, and she slips.

Duna is a kind of person he has never known before; Duna's life is ready-made for him.

She is five years older, a difference the same as her son's age. Little Gary, whose dad died three years ago, of a heart attack at the wheel of the blue-and-yellow delivery van he drove. He was only thirty-three.

Duna is half-Armenian. Tom isn't sure where Armenia is, whether it's still a real place on the map, but he likes this about Duna. It seems to account for her vibrancy, the blue-black colour of her hair, a great dark nest he can lose himself in and pretend he's a little bird. When she shakes him free of it the hair sprays out across the pillow, covering it like smoke.

On the airport bus there are a few backpackers: English, Canadian, two with Glasgow accents. The other people look dressed up by comparison. Whoever they are, they've turned into airline passengers, glad maybe of the special anonymity that lets only appearances describe them. He hasn't forgotten what a big adventure it was leaving Prestwick in that Jumbo. He'd had no fear of flying.

What will Jean be wearing?

This reminds him about the dress. When she wrote saying yes, he could have answered right away saying he'd had second thoughts. But he hadn't known then how involved he'd get with Duna. How could he? When he did decide to make a clean breast of it he got the letter telling him about the dress. Ivory silk. Esther had helped her make it. Esther would be coming out too, eventually, when they were settled.

There's an Indian family on the bus, the three women in brilliant glitter-edged saris, shaming the other passengers' anaemic summer wear. Duna has an oriental hanging on the wall of her apartment. She loves colour. There are drawings, pine shelves with books and plants, ceramic pots, woven samplers. Some of these she has made herself, others were gifts from people at the day-centre where she's an occupational therapist. Things she helped them to make. Duna's artistic. She can turn an ordinary room into another world. When he saw her apartment it was as if he had always been looking for a place like that to belong in, without ever having imagined it. He plays with the boy while Duna cooks; he washes the dishes afterwards. There's oriental music or jazz on the stereo.

It's too small for him to move in there, just one divided room, and the boy growing. They're looking together for a bigger apartment. He hasn't told Duna about Jean, only that an old girlfriend of his would be in town for a week or two. He sees the folly of this lie.

For a moment he holds his breath and almost prays, bowed to the fervent wish that Jean won't really mind when he tells her, that she'll see the sights and go back home without a fuss. And save her wedding dress for another time. It's a stupid wish. It occurs to him to claim a letter got lost in the post, telling her, that is.

He'll tell her at the airport. He'll take her out to dinner. He's found her a place to stay well away from Duna's. She'll be tired, jet-lagged. She could have a holiday, maybe fly out to that aunt and uncle in Vancouver. He would pay something towards the fare. He lights another cigarette, his hand shaking.

He is one of the first off the bus. He follows the yellow signs pointing up the escalator. The bar is crowded; he elbows his way in and orders a whisky. He has never been a drinker but he orders another one straight away. The alcohol sears his gut but it fails to unknot the panic setting in there, now that he is nearly face to face with her. The rain batters against the plate-glass windows. He's drowning in the sound of it, beseiged by other noises: the electronic tinkling that precedes announcements he can't make sense of, the thousand conversations dissolving in a hellish buzz. He watches other people waiting to meet flights and yields to an envy that is total, self-annihilating.

He sees her, still some way off behind the barrier, a laden trolley in front of her. She is looking for him, her face flushed with the eagerness of arrival. She is in blue. She seems young, from long ago and another time in his life.

When she reaches him she is radiant and he returns her long, tight hug, almost in tears. He is unaccustomed to whatever this feeling is. He tries to retreat from it. His first reaction is to forget he is meant to tell her now. When he remembers he knows he has to wait until the shock of emotion subsides.

On the bus she spills out stories of departure, of leaving this and that behind, of parties and gifts, and final goodbyes, and hailstones are smashing on the roof. Under the wheels there's a heavy rush of water that gets heavier and halfway to town they slow down on a stretch that's waterlogged completely. He can see nothing through the windows. The world outside is a distant aquarium.

The bus starts again. He lowers his head and puts his face in his hands. Jean touches his shoulder.

'Tom, are you all right?' And her voice is light and sweet, its breath of anxiety for him alone.

Over the Buda Hills . . .

I

*A woman, dark-lipped, watches as I sleep. Her face is a bruised
mask, her body straight as a reed. Her eyes glitter in a catalep-
tic stare, their colour lost. When she bends, sinuous, the air is cloying;
for she secretes in the crevices of elbows and knuckles, knees, armpits
and sex, the fragrant essences of figs and tulips, while the distilled
juices of orchids seep from her fingernails. Her hair is deepest black,
razor-edged against her shoulders; her breasts are small and tight like
pearls in the dark stretched sheen of her dress; her hips a steep and
never-ending slide of fingers. She is often there, and I have come to feel
she is me. Yet if she should touch me I would die, I know, of suffo-
cation.*

On waking I am filled with dread, then with revulsion for the
poisoning of my sleeping hours which this dream and its like
have brought. The incubi that meet me hugger-mugger in the
night. Sometimes I think they will drag me over the moat of

consciousness for ever. But they make my days endurable. Better to wake to fears that are soon dissipated than wake to loss that will never be. I have called up these monsters for that very reason.

At first I dreamt of Frank.

The doctor's pills helped me into easy sleep; there, seeking Frank and finding him, I was duped by consolation. But in the mornings I woke to the empty acres of my life, my life stripped of everything that made it life. So then I was drawn to everything that saved me from the freshness of living. I ignored all those thin and distant voices that crowded round my grief, warning me. What was morbid to them has become the air I swim in.

Like this, I neither remember nor forget. Everything remains in present tense. The planes of his face; his words, not the silence that surrounds me now.

It is our last whole day before he leaves. How I want to keep him by my side. But when he shakes his cigarette pack there is nothing left, and the shop is only steps away. As he walks down the path from the house, my eyes follow him, something sensed; perhaps a premonitory shiver. Minutes pass and I am back at the window, just as he turns the corner of Edwardes Lane. Then, in a tumult of time, seconds crashing into eternity, I see his death. Slowing, as if I could hold and stop the moment of it; yet I cannot. Everything is distinct: the car that skids crazily off the road, the huddling shape of a pink blanket that later covers him. And his umbrella. It has flown from his hand and lies crumpled and black, become a bird ready to take flight again, to abandon the dark wet pavement that has been his last foothold. Watching this, I lose the power to move.

Frank is now Ferenc, ever since his father's arrival.

He is a heavy man, his bulk persuasive, a natural source of the authority he displays. He takes his hat off when he enters the room, and his hair is smooth, meeting the high forehead in a sharp arrow point. His look is unwavering and when his eyes flood mine with their angry blue sorrow they remind me of Frank. They are Frank's eyes, Ferenc's eyes. They are wholly unforgiving, In them I find nothing for me but this. That I am the circumstance of his death.

When he leaves he shakes my hand, stiffly, with no kindness. He takes Frank's body with him.

I'll tell you about Frank, and how we met, and perhaps you'll see how much more I suffered from his father's stingy measure of my love. What is shared between two people has no need of days and months and years together in a room or a city.

It was September, one evening, at a friend's house. Judith. I hadn't seen Judith for a while — I'd been away — and when I had telephoned her the day before, she had invited me for dinner. Frank was there, a guest for the night, en route to Boston. Hardly more than changing planes.

When we smiled, it was with recognition, one of those luminous moments of certainty. Mysterious, yes, but simple. This kind of sudden love is transparent; without the shadow of a doubt.

After dinner we walked in Judith's long, narrow garden, and, standing by the high end wall where light poured from the kitchen window, we clinked our glasses. 'Good wine,' he said, dipping a finger in it and touching my lips It was as close as we came to a kiss that night.

In the early morning, when I thought of his plane far above the Irish Sea, I hadn't a care.

Then came our letters; an unforeseen reward for patient separation. How little I realised I would come to value them.

By the time Frank was back in London for Christmas we knew each other with a lulled knowledge that would now be released into full, quick perceptions – of each other, and everything. Love lifting us out of the world, and returning us to it with not five but a hundred senses; the world of euphoria, where every sight and sound and touch is amplified.

Our bodies merged, not only in love, but in sleep, for we turned to one another in the same moments of the night and found our dreams had synchronicity. Lying beside him, searching for the outlines of his face in shadow, I was overcome with the silence and the nearness of him: each breath he breathed was mine too; I felt the rise and fall of his lungs from within; I entered the pulsing of his heart and shared his skin. Our touch was simultaneous. When we talked we tried to remember our separate pasts entire, for the sake of giving everything into each other's possession.

We walked the canal tow-path and wandered over Hampstead Heath, only too happy to lose our way, scornful of time and direction, sure of the charmed randomness that had led us together. On Christmas Day we ate a goose that Frank had searched for as the shops were closing and found by some miracle in an Islington butcher's where it had been ordered and never claimed. On New Year's Eve we drank champagne and made the new decade ours. We were exiles who had found a country that was ours alone. Had ours not been a winter love, the sun might have turned us more towards the world; but that, we thought, was still to come. For now, the dazzle was all inside.

Terrible things are unconvincing. My inability to believe what had happened meant estrangement from the world as it was.

There was no light in a world that did not contain Frank, and the darkness around me bred morbid longings. It was in books that I found the means of nourishing them. I read poems of love and death. I turned to Poe and the poets who admired him; I embraced their obsessions with decadent dreams and the taste of corruption. I took books from the library where I work, tearing out their images, I pinned these to my bedroom walls, and every inch was soon covered in offerings to the lady of death, she and her cohorts mirrored there. The moonlight gleam of teeth out of a shadow mask, the lure of wrath-filled milky eyes, the raking hands with spider claws, the purple lips imparting deadly kisses, the hair that casts a drowning web upon a riverbank; the furred or feathered beasts that crouch and suck and cling, the murderess with the rose of blood upon her guilty palms, dark-angel wings enfolding like a shroud, quick reptile tongues of lethal flame, a ravaged ship upon a siren shore . . . In my clearer hours I was sickened by these things, the foul howling creatures and devouring women, distorted and triumphant. But so long as I lived and Frank was dead, I knew I was doomed to be one of them. I bore the burden of his fate. I was the occasion of his death.

With my passage into these tenebrous regions came a con-suming fear of the sunlight. It must have been several days that I sat in the curtained flat, having sealed every mouth of light, having patched the keyholes and the letterbox opening. I was rescued, in delirium they said.

In hospital recovery came. Abandoned and stricken as I was, without close family, I responded to nurture, feeling like a child, helpless but being cared for, newly innocent.

Before I left, a white-coated woman doctor talked to me about the necessity for mourning, about the painful stages of separation from someone who has died, and I took heed, for the first time hopeful of life, hopeful of hope, no longer lost in grief's deep cave, in wastes of sickly devastation.

Months passed, I returned to my job at the library, and though I was still very thin, with shadows on my cheeks, a flickering vitality returned. Spring arrived and it gave me heart. I welcomed the sun on my face. One afternoon I sat with Judith in her garden, where the blue scabious were in bloom and an amber-eyed kitten lay at our feet, and I told her that I had turned my back on death. That night I dreamt a new dream, still troubling but unlike all the rest.

A town of deserted streets, of locked doors and shuttered windows, and white flags flying from every gabled rooftop. This dream of surrender is bleached and flat, its texture papery. Until now they have been dreams of greater density, frames to be entered, containing infinite interior space whose emanations seek me out. Here I am only a spectator. I watch the landscape scorch and crumble, its remnants flutter towards vanishing point. And then a night of dreamless, uninvaded sleep. The first.

I knew white too is mourning's colour, and I wept. It was

a new season for me. Although everything now was muted, bereft of the eloquence that lovers listen for, the rattle of the pebbles on the distant shore.

It is late summer, and almost a year from the day when I first met Frank. When that day comes I read all his letters. They seem to tell me that now I must travel to Budapest. I write to Frank's father. Judith and my other friends try to dissuade me from going alone.

II

Five o'clock on Christmas Eve and Ferihegy airport is hushed and gleaming with desertion, its bright empty concourse like the middle of the night. The first signs of strangeness excite me: the forest-green uniforms, the hermetic words that bar my path with exclamations. As the bus crosses the ill-lit suburbs the sun sets and everything darkens. The darkness is thick and unrelieved. At Engles Square, in the darkest city I have known, I take a taxi.

At the door to the gloomy dining-room a man in hotel livery murmurs that his staff are all spending this holiday night at home and there is no one left to serve food. A buffet is laid out instead. On my crimson tablecloth a shaded candle burns. The liveried overseer brings a glass of wine. Red wine, thick like blood beside the candle's yellow glow, and in the glass there seems to burn a flame of secret life. At first I do not drink and merely sit there, tired and mesmerised, then my hand reaches out.

It seems I am alone, until I catch the sound of German voices and I turn to see an elderly couple seated in the shadows of a corner. Hard in this light to name the food I've dished on to my plate. Though its peppery flavours tantalise, I find I have no appetite. My head aches and my throat feels dry and prickly.

All the same, I venture out, a warm scarf swathing my neck and ears, to walk at least to the end of the street. I crave a glimpse of the city's life. I am loath to sleep without having this, some small embrace of arrival.

Deserted pavements. Only the bounce of sound my own footsteps make. A church I come to has its doors flung open. In the porch a notice in German and Hungarian announces sung mass at midnight. Inside, there is no one; just the fragrance of incense and altar lilies, and, by the crib, the resiny pungence of the fir trees huddled round it. The lights looped across their branches make the emptiness friendly and expectant. I close my eyes and stand for a while breathing in this Christmas-scented air, inhaling solace, as if I could store it in my lungs.

The weather's mildness takes me by surprise. I had been prepared for icy temperatures, foreseeing chilled air and snow underfoot, rather than this suave dampness seeping from the Danube. How far I am from the sea; how locked in by land.

Christmas Day. I plan to telephone them later in the morning. The answer to my letter lies smoothed flat on the dressing-table; polite, noncommital, opaque as a stone. Though surely they'll agree to meet me now, now that I am here.

I set out early to explore this part of the city. Here I am in the Váci Utca shopping centre where people stroll in couples and slow holiday bunches; fidgety teenagers, loden-clad families with children and grandparents. A thin fog billows above the white Christmas lights that drape the street. It clings to the top of a tall art nouveau building, swirling past its decorative gilt, suddenly making me think of a Klimt painting.

Värösmärty Square has a giant Christmas tree at its centre. Standing beside it, quite alone, is a stocky middle-aged man in a fur hat and a sheepskin jacket. He holds a goggle-eyed tape deck that is playing the overture from *The Magic Flute*, very loud, and as I pass him he slips a slyly intimate smile at me. I wonder for a moment if he is someone I know.

Over the Danube, fog obscures the water, silencing it, the pervading dampness the muffled river's only sign. I now have sure symptoms of a cold. Sniffing, moist-eyed, I retreat into my turned-up collar. With no one else in sight, I make my way along the Danube promenade. A yellow tram rattles past me out of the mist; then, just as suddenly, it is gone, and the riverside tracks it followed disappear with it, fog-blurred behind a fence. I look towards the hazy outline of the Buda Hills; Frank told me he often liked to go there, to walk in the trees far above the city. Down here the morning is stunned, windless.

When I telephone a woman answers. It's not a young voice; not his sister. I start by saying the family's name, then give mine and in English tell her where I'm staying. She seems not to understand. I try a little German, but before I get all the words out the line goes dead.

I wait a few minutes and try again; this time Frank's father answers. Almost at once he says they'll meet me at my hotel at half-past five. His voice is offhand, effortlessly abrupt, and when I blurt a suggestion to visit them at home he cuts it short and says that won't be necessary.

It is nearly twelve now and time for lunch, for I had no appetite for breakfast and I need to eat to stop myself from feeling tired. In a half-empty restaurant close to the hotel I order chicken paprika and swallow a few morsels. At the next table two blonde women are chewing their food slowly between languid pauses. They have creamy complexions and features whose heaviness is luxuriant rather than coarse. I've noticed this same sensuality in the faces of other women on the street. It strikes me that though Frank was fair and blue-eyed I had half expected the women to be dark like me. Once, my Polish neighbour Krysha had told me I resembled a Hungarian princess.

I had appeared that evening in a new dress: wine-coloured, with a gathered calf-length skirt. She said it went with my hair (it was long and wavy at that time), and the paleness of my 'delicate' face, in a way that reminded her of fragile Habsburg ladies. This compliment made a seductive impression on me; it stirred the memory of girlhood fantasies that I wasn't really who I thought I was.

The christening of my 'Hungarian dress' must have been about a year before I met Frank.

I try hard to rid myself of the thought that he is waiting for me somewhere here, but it persists.

I am on a bus crossing the Danube and the fog has cleared a little since this morning. At the start of the cogwheel railway there is a train already in the station. After minutes waiting for more passengers to board, it lurches off suddenly up towards the Széchenyi Hill. Frosted evergreens lean against the steep track, scrawling a lacy screen across the moving windows.

Then, as the train gains speed, the whole landscape of copses and villa gardens drops away in sparkling sunlit tiers.

But at the hilltop terminus the sun has faded behind dense, chilling fog. Some passengers make their way across the platform, towards what I take to be a road, and at once they dwindle out of sight. Others walk, dreamily it seems, across the small square, as if waiting for the fog to lift at any moment. The rest converge on a mobile drinks stand in the corner by the station.

I turn towards the trees. What I want most is solitude, somewhere beyond this foggy enclosure suspended in the time between trains.

When I reach the tree-line I look back and can no longer see a soul; just a cobweb veil of grey.

The stillness comforts. I am sorely drawn to the pale and quiet hills that I imagine lie ahead. I would like to walk there, invisible, with only the fog for company; yet its dangers deter me and I see myself its solid centre, to be hugged by it and tightly bound in vapour. Lingering among the trees I soon begin to shiver from the damp and know it's best to go back and get warm again, though when I move to leave, for a moment something makes me falter.

People are drifting to the station now. I hurry to the drinks stand, where there is only a man in a dark-green loden, being handed a miniature glass of what looks like brandy. I point to his drink; the woman nods and at once pours one for me. She wears fingerless gloves and must have thick layers beneath her blue overall, for she shows no sign of feeling cold. As soon as I gulp the spirit down, glad of its burning sweetness, I start to cough.

The brandy has made me sweat and, slumped in the train again, I have become heavy-headed, only longing to crawl into bed. Although we go down at a dizzying speed, the driver dithers at each of the stops. At last, in my room, I swallow two aspirins and sleep for an hour, fitfully.

When I wake and dress I feel better, convinced my temperature is back to normal. But something is snagging on my memory, something to do with Frank that I never knew before, learned and then forgotten as I slept. All the way down in the lift it is like an itch.

I see them when I step into the foyer, all three of them. I watch for a moment before moving towards them; the two women sitting opposite Frank's father, their backs turned to me, the severity of his face.

Márta surveys me with moderate curiosity. Harder to bear is the cordial reserve of Mrs Heller's greeting when her husband makes the introductions: her head tilted back, then down in a nod almost long enough and slow enough to count as a bow. Márta speaks some English, but says little. All our words shrivel against the adjacent clatter of the bar service and the din of the television, where a group of young tourists are watching pop videos. Already disappointed, I wonder why they chose this spot when there are more secluded foyer alcoves empty.

After I take some snapshots of me and Frank from my bag and set them on the table there is a stern silence. The photographs lie there, shockingly glossy, waiting to be picked up, but no one touches them. At last Mrs Heller gazes down at the wintry images of her smiling son by my side. We are in

Judith's Twickenham garden again, by the wall, under a leaf-
less plane tree.

A moment later she looks up and gives me a brief stare, as
if seeing me for the first time. I realise how different I must
seem from that other, glowing face in front of her. I feel the
nausea of self-pity and I want to cry, but I stop myself, knowing that tears would enact an excessive claim on Frank.

I bring out the letters. Mr Heller glances at these and nods.
Márta turns to me, beginning to form a question, then has
second thoughts. Her mother fingers an envelope and squints
at the US stamp. 'M.I.T.,' she says, the English pronunciation
strangely clear, and gives me the start of a smile. 'Yes, M.I.T.,'
I add, my smile answering hers, and for a few moments we
look at one another, she with keener eyes than mine.

The emotion that sits on this mute exchange dissolves
when Mr Heller glances up at the clock and drinks a conclu-
sive mouthful of coffee. There's a prompt shuffling of chairs,
the waiter is paid and my hand shaken in three slight movements whose peremptory formality startles me. But, as her
parents are swept into the dark street beyond the revolving
doors, Márta steps back and takes my hand once more.

'I'll come again . . . maybe I'll call you first.'

Exhaustion drives me straight to bed. Willingly, I give way
to illness, for my temperature is up again. If I take more
aspirins and sweat out the fever it will be gone by morning.
My few days here are too precious to lose. They are for me to
see Frank's Budapest.

In the middle of a feverish night, I stagger to the bathroom.
Before getting back into bed I go to the window and lift

back the curtain. Nothing to see: misty rooftops, darkness
diluted only by the single streetlamp far below. But I feel a
sudden closeness to Frank, as if he and I were the only wake-
ful inhabitants of the city. I listen for something. There's only
the stillness, which is absolute – not a footfall, not a car to be
heard. And that's enough. It tempts me to open the window
and I pull at the metal edge of the glass panel. Behind it
there's another: double glazing. The catch is just out of my
reach, the effort too much for me.

What I've listened for seems to be answered in the hot,
shivery tangle of sleep and non-sleep. Frank is there, a nearer,
more intense presence than in dreams. He takes my hand and
together in the fog we cross the Danube. On we walk, up
through the cobbled streets of the old town, then higher and
higher, into the Buda Hills, until at last, true sublunary lovers,
all the tiredness from our journey falling from us, we enter a
brilliant monochrome forest whose frost-whitened branches
are clad in ripe moonlight. They caress us both, the cold fingers of these long, pale, satin-sleeved arms. They wind
themselves around us.

Around eight I wake, cooler and clear-headed.

At ten, I am on a packed tourist bus, and our sightseeing
guide is late. Into a hubbub of polyglot complaints I cough in
stifled spasms, until the restless Greeks and Germans and
shrugging Californians begin to spill out, and I join them. It
seems like fate that in the next bay stands a bus about to leave
for Hüvösvölgy. Soon I'm on my way across to Buda, jolting
up beyond the city; almost to the high meadows. Seen from
above, Pest has succumbed to the fog.

Once I am outside, the thin air takes my breath away and I splutter, gasping against the catch in my chest. When I become more accustomed I start walking, through a pure and silent landscape, its silvered trees making it seem enchanted, held by the onset of fairy-tale time.

After a while I stop to rest at one of the wooden picnic tables planted in clearings near the path. Tiredness makes me sink my head in my arms and I lean forward on to the frost-engraved wood. It is peaceful here and I am happy I came, but I know I should have asked about returning to the city. I don't want to stay out in the cold for long.

Yet I find it hard to get up to go back towards the village, and when I do, feeling revived, I am drawn towards the woods and their ethereal calm. It is now, stepping between the trees, that I feel I am no longer alone. There is no one in sight, no sound to signal another presence, just my sense that someone is moving through the wood ahead of me, and instead of making me uneasy this urges me forward.

I quicken my pace, faster, faster, breathlessly, forgetting cold and warmed by eagerness. But I fail to catch up with him; the further I go on, the more I am convinced it's a man who is in front of me. And that when I finally reach him he will be Frank. Or, if not Frank, someone, a living person, very like him. Time and circumstance are being conjugated here into a special tense, a chink between past and future through which anything can pass. It strikes me all at once that many things in our lives may be predestined, so that there is a shape to them, a fit between our heart's desire and what happens to us. This means there's perfection to start with – like the clear beauty of young children – but then things go awry:

accidents, small failures, being in the wrong place, miniscule changes that can pervert the unformed plan from its course. My first meeting with Frank was a confirmation of the real possibility of rightness. (But how fragile and vulnerable we are.) Now, here, I feel I may be close to it again. I think I'm going north, for the sun, listless and flat whenever it appears, is behind me.

Then the spell is broken. I have walked a long way and I am weary again, coughing, reluctant to go on. There is nowhere to rest – only the cold ground, bald and frost-hard.

It takes a long time to find my way back. Although there is no sound behind me, from having been the eager hunter I worry now that I've become the prey. The road, when I reach it, is empty. Ten minutes later a bus looms into view and I consider it a lucky rescue.

At the hotel I find a note from Márta asking me to meet her that afternoon at the Café Gerbeaud. The invitation restores my spirits and convinces me that all I need is a rest and some sleep. Despite this, once I'm in bed, swaddled in blankets and in the curtained gloom, I feel such a weight on my head and chest, and such a sinking into loneliness, that I am unable to picture myself ever leaving this room again, far less ever reaching Várösmärty Square.

The bed becomes a dark pit, moist and inescapable, sucking me in, holding me back from knowing Frank's city and holding me back from Frank himself, out there waiting for me to discover him, free and light. I writhe in the grip of longing for a well-being that seems already too remote. How am I to brace myself against the soft, unfeeling space of the streets, with no touch to steady me, no hand to hold mine, until I should reach him.

At last I sleep. I wake at five, damp with sweat, but my temperature down; I have a perfunctory wash and struggle into my clothes.

The deserted square makes the chandelier-lit windows of Gerbeaud's all the more inviting. Not one free table is left and I am too bewildered by the mêlée of faces to pick out Márta's, until I notice a raised arm waving in the distance, in the second room beyond the door.

We order coffee with cakes. My fingers tremble as I stir the foamy liquid, and I dare not look straight into Márta's eyes. But among the smoky, chattering crowd with hats and overcoats piled all around, it is as if I have reached some place of safety, become at last one of the city's compacted atoms, no longer stray and floating.

Márta's questions: all with that reserve I have come to expect here; yet searching, circling, asking for a share in the singular knowledge I had of Frank.

My questions: so much simpler on the surface; I want a narrative of family and childhood, of a face altering into manhood, of a life far beyond my existence, yet lived moving towards me. And I want the heart of her memories, envy and fear as well as tenderness, rivalry as well as love. Although this, I know, is asking too much.

Her answers don't barter emotions for confidences, but lay them bare as my due, as her brother's. This surprises me, it seems unstinting, and in her generosity I find immense relief. We look at one another then, as if stumbling on some earlier, forgotten curiosity, and I am sure that she begins to see me,

me myself, absolved of her brother's death. I am pulled tight
into the present, the past jerking away from me as I receive
this absolution.

Time and again, our conversation is broken by my cough,
now made worse in the smoky atmosphere. Márta begins to
insist that I see a doctor. I protest that there's no need.

She arrives early next morning to see how I am.

I've felt bad in the night, and my fatigue now is like the aftermath of a battle, a battle with delirium and against the
constriction in my chest, the weight of my limbs and head, as if
they were bound to something leaden beneath them; it seemed
that only by constant movement could I prevent them falling
into paralysis. And so I flailed and wrestled with the sheets,
twisting my face and neck against the flattened pillows, my eyes
burning, the space behind them molten. All the terrible fires of
dream become physical, conquering my consciousness.

Frank was there, a stronger presence than ever, pitying me,
watching my struggle from the foot of the bed, soothing me,
his voice urgent and caressing, pleading to help me, to free
me, to love me again, drawing me towards him with fierce,
hungry whispers.

Only when I found the strength to call out, though my cry
can have been no more than a hoarse complaint – 'Go away,
Frank, please leave me' – did I lapse into healing sleep.

Márta tells me the doctor is on his way.

This doctor's cure is the banal sanity of diagnosis.
Bronchitis.

He purses his lips. 'Go outside and I promise you
pneumonia.'

He looks at me severely and his thick-lensed spectacles seem to mist up, but I am the one still in the fog. Heavy, bald, around fifty, a thick accent that sounds almost stagey — like an intellectual on the run from the Nazis in an old Hollywood film. It makes me feel better to be told, by such a man, that I am really ill; a secure loss of responsibility. He and Márta are now my guardian angels.

Eyes streaming, lips cracking from the effort, I force a smile to both of them.

Then it dawns on me that I may miss my flight tomorrow. My heart beats out a warning at the thought of being stranded in this city, and for how long? I know I have to catch that plane and I tell the doctor so, weakly conveying desperation. He sighs and adds a yellow box to the pile now assembled on my bedside table. 'These are for just before the plane.'

He goes to the window.

'You really should keep warm.'

Pulling back the curtain, he snaps shut the double glass panels which someone must have left open yesterday. Perhaps the chambermaid.

In the course of that day Márta comes and goes, a benign shadow interpolated in my sleep, making sure I swallow the long thin capsules of penicillin, feeding me dark brown syrup with a plastic spoon that feels oddly formless on my tongue. What I touch, taste and hear still seems indistinct from me, as if I have melted into it. I yearn to wrench myself away, to be me alone, sure within the confines of my body. Yet this yielding is so sweet.

My night is less troubled than the one before, but fevered,

and again I'm in the forest, pursued in a cloud of silence, not a twig snapping, nor a whirring wing, and Frank is calling that he'll rescue me. I run.

In the morning I breathe more easily, my limbs have lightened, become looser, and the thick mesh on my vision has lifted. Márta arrives early to help me dress and pack. I watch her move about the room, her smiles and gestures impressed upon me by the gentle new clarity of things. Now her presence contains faint but sure echoes of her brother, of the flesh and blood Frank that I loved.

Fuzzy with medicines, I am taken to the airport by the Hellers. They are kind, all three of them; Frank's parents perhaps a little too kind, their kindness kindled by guilt, and a tinge of fear, as if I'll ask them to admit they have wronged me. But Márta is devoid of this.

She is soon to be married and I wish her well. As I enter the customs lane I turn to wave to them and she is thoughtful, her unsmiling expression now reminding me emphatically of Frank, although she is dark and not at all like him.

She seems not to see me at all, and then she waves.

Virgins

White sand, glinting with mica, and the cobalt sky washed pale by bands of cirrus. A blowy spring sun that licks my back hot for ten minutes then leaves me in the lurch, goose-pimples rising, until the cloud passes.

This light gives the water a sheer diamond sparkle, but at the push of final distance creamy little waves rush out of the calm, hitting the shore in commotions of spray. It's too cold here at the ocean's edge. I've dipped a toe and that's enough; I'm not a hardy swimmer.

I breast the land instead, reaching wide, gathering sand, then opening my fists to let it fly. Pearly grains get caught in my nails; flimsy abrasions in the soft finger clefts becoming magnified, points of definition as I drowse inside the fuzz of sound and colour.

Rolling over, I fill one hand, and let the warm fine sand drip and slide on my stomach.

Slowly. I'm waiting.

I have no idea where he's gone. To get cigarettes? A news-paper? When we had walked across and picked out our sunbathing spot he turned on his heel as if he'd forgotten something. Be right back; the words were thrown behind him.

When I think of that beach I'm alone on it with two lines of footprints. But he must have been there some of the time. Was it on the second day he took the photograph of me looming against the water and the sky, dishevelled, looking tall, which I'm not, and with an angled shadow making me lopsided? He must have been lying flat, my camera tilted up at me. Maybe acting as if he was teasing, only pretending to take a picture.

It was Holy Week and we were there for three days. Did we go to Huelva or didn't we?

My memory's hazy. Or rather it isn't. I have a clear mem-ory, but I'm not certain it's a real one, perhaps just what he told me we would see if we went. Like a persistently remem-bered dream. The procession leaving the church, shuffling across the square in the full glare of spotlights, pressing into the narrow streets where the tall, snake-flamed candles cast tapering shadows on the walls. More sinister than sacred.

And the other *penitentes* in their pointed hoods, heaving and sweating under the great weight of the float that carries the polychrome Virgin, canopied, larger and more vivid than life, with her rouged cheeks and her carmined lips and the frozen glass teardrops beneath her forget-me-not gaze. She's wearing a collar of gold and amethysts, and earrings swing about her face as the *paso* staggers forward, swaying. What those men won't do for her as she sits up there all painted and holy. Strained shoulders and torn tendons in the neck. Slipped discs.

Guapa! Guapa! Guapa!

The crowd gets overexcited seeing her go by. Enrique had told me that sometimes men from different parishes fight over their local Virgins, defend their beauty, insult their rivals, even call each others' Virgins whores. Or daughters of whores, or whores who shit on their mothers.

Yes, now I'm sure we went, and I really did see the procession. I remember drinking *fino* with *tapas* in a dingy little bar down by the port, a place that reeked of *anís* and stale fish oil. I remember it because we had an argument. Huelva was ugly. It looked as if it had been ugly for a long time, nothing to do with modernity.

But the beach is beautiful. Long and flat, shady trees behind it. Umbrella pines I think they were. Or were they tamarisks? Columbus sailed past here, Enrique told me, down the estuary and round this prong of land, out into the pristine ocean to find America. It was why he'd brought me there; that and a memory of a childhood holiday.

Now the sun has come out again in earnest, and I shake the sand off my tummy as a bar of heat presses down on it. I think about the night before and about waking that morning beside him. Him. Him in syncopated close-ups. Arms, legs, mouth, skin, the swell of his ribcage as he lies on his back, the high curve of a nostril in profile. And the sweetness of us clamped together. I see him staring at me in the shower with that slatey, almost jealous look, saying he has always dreamed about a girl like me, blonde hair and blue eyes. I'm lucky; blonde-ness circumvents so many imperfections.

When he does come back I don't hear him. My eyes are shut. I feel a breath in my ear, a finger tickle on the hollow of my throat. I sigh and expect a kiss. No kiss. So I open my eyes and see him stretching out on the sand just far enough away from me not to be in touching distance. There's an elbow pointed in my direction, but his face is held to the sun.

I want the sun to get back behind a cloud.

'Where have you been?'

'Nowhere in particular.'

He doesn't even blink. The sound of the little waves marks time for me, a moment lost with each beat on the shore. I sit up and give an ostentatious shiver that gets me nowhere.

For a while I rest my eyes on the heavy dark blue line of the horizon, its pull a release from his tantrum. If that's what it is.

As we drink our beers in the harbour café he is polite, solicitous about the sea breezes. He drapes his jacket about my sleeveless shoulders. When I asked him this morning why he wore trousers with button-flies he said zips were not for gentlemen. He's no older than me and I am only twenty.

I know about his family background, his mother gave me a lesson in peeling oranges. With a knife and fork.

So now we're becalmed, the body's shared secrets overboard and intimacy deserting us. For the rest of the day I'm mocked by his good manners.

Then all at once his anger bursts. Damn you. Shut up. Tell me. Nothing to tell that he didn't know before. But he calls me whore, daughter of whore, though he spares me whore who shits on her mother. At first I can't believe my ears.

That night we make love, me in spite of myself. I'm glad

the light is out and it's over soon. I turn from the moonlight that pierces the blind. Sleep comes, deep and dreamless.

I am hauled out of it by the weight of his body moving on mine.

In the moonlit dark I can see his face, the eyes closed; his breathing tells me he is not awake. His skin burns and the hairs on it feel furry as they rub against me. I want to scream but instead I yield. Sleeping, he is awesomely immoveable. I lie on the other side of a nightmare's paralysis, my body not numbed but lucid in the face of what's impervious. And yet, there's pleasure.

When I tell him in the morning he is shaving, foam on his cheeks and chin, and I'm watching through the little bathroom's open door. He laughs at first, disbelieving, but as he draws in his mouth to scrape above the upper lip I can see contempt slur across his mirrored eyes. And then a smile of fathomless satisfaction.

There has been only one lover before him, but now that I've become his rite of passage I'm looser and more dangerous than the girl he knew a week ago. Because he's the boy virgin just over the threshold, needing to claim a man's mistrust of women. Most of all he is angry because he will always remember me.

There are apologies, bouts of sullen tenderness, the trip to Huelva. But I've had enough and I cross the Guadiana into Portugal. He drives me there and I wave goodbye as the ferry slips across, watching the Spanish bank until I can't see him any more. I like a stretch of water for a frontier. No turning back until you are truly on the other side, already somewhere new.

The boat glides low and flat like a raft; me there standing on the deck, waiting hard, watching the river make for the sea, holding my breath for arrival.

My heart must have been beating very fast.

F Stands for Freedom

Ireland tilts eastward at the top, ready to fall where Scotland pokes out quivering, misshapen fingers, contours almost matching up across the Mull of Galloway. If you stick to that Irish coast and run your eye south round a corner or two, you soon arrive in Newry. Now look back.

This is Newry; a busy town. It straddles the counties of Down and Armagh, it crowns the long neck of Carlingford Lough and the Armagh mountains rise dark at its back. Misty or clear-topped, they give the place beneath them a sense of singular location; that scale of low and high once so vital to painters and photographers when measuring the human in a landscape. Down there, on board the ships that slip into Newry's bustling canal, there is English corn, American cotton via Liverpool, slates from the South Wales quarries, and coal. Coal from the mines of Lanarkshire and Ayrshire, the Rhondda Valley and Lancashire; coal which gives the dockers of Newry a brotherhood of the skin with the colliers over the

Channel. Of the shipping that leaves and ploughs away east through the lough, some vessels sail out light, but many carry ropes and sails and grass seed, or have holds weighed low with local granite. Day in, day out, the movement of goods churns at the waves and black trails of steam blunt their surface. Newry is a prosperous town, for those with the means to prosper in this first summer of the century's last decade.

Rose Tierney is one of those who do not. She is thirty-three and her looks put her well past forty. She has given birth to seven children, four of whom survive. Gerald is eleven, Catherine eight, Elizabeth Anne is four, and there is Alfie, the baby, thriving again after croup and fever in the winter; a recovery owing, his mother believes, to the intervention of Saint Anthony in response to a novena. Rose is a small, stocky woman with dark hair whose greying strands curl out from under the frayed and discoloured flannel scarf she wears indoors and out. She has a fine pair of eyes, a hazel that lightens to green in the sunlight. She has a short temper and a manner so abrupt it gives some cause to avoid her.

She was Rose McGinn until she married Michael Tierney, and her family farmed at Carnlough. She has worked on the land all her life. Ten years have passed since that farm of her childhood was lost, and only yesterday Michael Tierney too had notice of eviction.

They have nine acres, one rood and five perches, a cow and four hens and after three months, they have passed the sacred limit for arrears of rent. What will they do? Plans have to be made; today the question Michael is asking himself is when is it best to sell the cow.

★

Newry in 1890 strives to believe it is a town of men in frock-coats and respectable merchants, of clean-fingered traders and pale decorous ladies, who, with the benefit of elocution lessons, crimp their mouths when they enunciate West British vowels, and hold their cheeks in hard so they sound altogether less Irish than their husbands and brothers and fathers. Dirt, however, thwarts some of these drawing-room aspirations. Who can avoid it? Coal dust floats up from the quays and spreads through the town at the least breath of wind, to mix with all the muck of agricultural traffic. Three times weekly market soils the streets; cow-pats and pig-shit and the carts going up and down all add to the everyday horse-dung underfoot; certain well-frequented footpaths, what is more, remain in a sorry state of disrepair. The ladies' hems get rimmed with filth. Sewerage pipes and mains drainage are yet to be extended to many localities. The town stinks, in summer most of all.

The eggs collected by Catherine and Elizabeth Anne are taken by Rose to Saturday's market. Three of them, though, are saved for after mass on Sunday. With the money from the eggs, and a pail of buttermilk she took along with them, Rose buys tea, lamp oil and a quarter pound of soap for the washing. Before the walk home she goes to her brother's house on Hill Street, where earlier she had left Elizabeth Anne. Joe McGinn is out delivering coal and Rose finds her mother with Cissy, who is reading her a letter, a long-awaited letter from Desmond in America. The old lady is no illiterate; long ago at the hedge school she learned how to read, and she even knows some Latin, but her eyesight is failing badly. Desmond is one of her two youngest sons, twins who emigrated just a year ago to Boston He is doing grand and there is money with the letter, a piece of news that at once emboldens Rose. She turns to her sister-in-law: 'I know you haven't much, but if you could spare me a wee poke of sugar, I can pay you back next week.'

With a smile of reassurance – or is it satisfaction? – Cissy McGinn takes a sheet of saved brown paper from the scullery press and, holding it against the table's edge, tears off an even-sided piece which she deftly folds to a cone shape. Into it she pours the sugar, careful not to spill a single granule, then folds the paper's pointed end across and tucks it in. Rose calls to Elizabeth Anne, who is playing in the yard with her cousins. She will keep the sugar poke and return with it brimful the following Saturday.

Desmond and Tom McGinn were among seventy thousand that Ireland lost to emigration in 1889. In the fifty years before that, hunger, dispossession and despair drove over three million across the Atlantic and the Irish Sea; more than half the country's population, though some were only corpses when they reached their journey's end. The Famine that killed in the forties still attends on the wait for each harvest, and this summer the prospect of a failed potato crop is a matter for concern. There is blight in Cavan and Donegal West and Fermanagh, though in Down and Armagh the crop seems safe, except for certain cases of tubers found diseased in boggy soil.

Potatoes are needed to feed the peasants and the Newry poor; their betters have a different cause for worry. At a meeting in Monaghan Street the millers' union votes to fight for shorter hours in mills owned by Walker's, O'Hagen's and Beattie's. Unloading has been much disrupted by agitation and disputes on the quays at Dublin Bridge and Albert Basin, and the Union of Dock Labourers has a membership swelling in the Newry branch. At the Home Rule Hall in Castle Street, thirty new members joined this week, bringing its numbers to close on three hundred. Strikes are reported elsewhere in Ireland, and in Phoenix Park a trades meeting takes place in furtherance of the eight hours movement.

These are mere ripples from across the water, where Labour is well and truly on the march. The land has bred resistance in Ireland. In England, Wales and Scotland the soil of organised industry has grown fertile of late, its victories already being harvested.

Newry's great and good: the Town Commission, the Board of Guardians, the Reverends this-and-that all suffer consternation at the frequent breaking of the peace. Rowdiness intrudes on their sleep; it rakes their clear consciences. Late on Saturday night last, a gang of roughs, filled with mean whiskey by the sound of them, started out to sack the town in the precincts of Mill Street and William Street. Smashing windows, ripping shutters off their hinges and wrecking a cart that stands in their unsteady way. Yet the constabulary was nowhere near to check their wildness. A mystery. Earlier that night in the High Street, a brawl, as regular, breaks out between the Hogans and McCartneys, and there they are, truncheons at the ready in a flash. Could the midnight marauders have been soldiery? Incidents abound after dark when they harass, even injure the citizens. On Merchant's

Quay, a trio of redcoats, privates from the Third East
Lancashires, swagger into O'Hare's public house, all of them
the worse for drink to start with. When they ask to be served
they are refused and ugly anti-Irish words are flung across the
counter. Mrs O'Hare protests. One of the unwelcome visitors
leans across and spits into her face. A labourer who leaves to
find the police, fearing for the safety of the house and its cus-
tomers, is pursued and beaten with a soldier's belt.

Drunk or sober, it is not uncommon for army and police to
be refused by publicans on principle. Rent boycotts continue,
condemned though they are by the Holy See, and the gaols
still slam their doors on those convicted of opposing eviction
under the Coercion Act.

Daylight Newry's middle class is buttoned up but has its
pleasures. The Lawn Tennis Club holds its annual tourna-
ment to a large and fashionable gathering of spectators, despite
the showery weather. In the final of the ladies' singles Miss
Magee beats Miss Booth three to six, seven to five, six to
four, and wins a gold and pearl brooch as her prize. On
steamer sailings to Greenore and Warrenpoint excursions the
ladies and gentlemen mingle with the rougher Sunday crowds.
In Margaret Square, at Warnock's Stationers and Bookshop,
preserve labels are purchased and orders placed for calling
cards. The summer's new books are on window display and in
pride of central place sit the two lavish volumes of Mr
Stanley's famed *In Darkest Africa*.

Rose Tierney could weep she is so weary, but she mutters
small complaints instead. It took Michael nearly all forenoon

to sell the cow and when he came back she walked to market with Gerald to sell the last of the buttermilk and a stone of good potatoes newly dug. Now in the dwindling light she is back at the ridges to salvage what she can from the patch of moory ground before the cottage, where the crop is poorer, partly blighted.

Tomorrow they expect the bailiff and his men, so Rose has had to go visiting and be visited by her neighbours, to say goodbyes and hand on things they won't be carrying with them: the old churn she brought from Carnlough, the rake and the spade and the big zinc washtub . . . They have all found something to give her in return: a pound of oats, a muffler for Gerald, an old carpet-bag that will come in handy, some unripe apples she knows were picked by children from branches overhanging the Wilsons' high wall. Nothing grows on the stunted trees that border Rose and Michael's field. Rose doesn't even know the names of them; she never learned the names of trees, only bushes, from berrying.

She straightens up, rubbing the soreness on her back, when she sees Michael coming towards her on the road, along with Hughie Noonan. Michael has been out visiting too, to see Father Doherty and one or two others. When the men reach the cottage Hughie offers Michael a smoke and Rose goes inside. The children, all but Gerald, are asleep, and she sits looking out through the open top half of the door, watching the reddened sky get darker,

It is the quietness that strikes her in the morning. With the cow gone and the hens given to Cissy and Joe in part payment for the passage money, the animal sounds she has started the day with for years have deserted her.

She boils what there is of the potatoes while the children have their breakfast, then she wraps up the food they will all carry with them. She sweeps the floor after Michael hefts the heavy bundles out. He is taking these to Noonan's to save them from the bailiff. Along with blankets and dishes and pots she packed the clock that was her father's and the *Lives of the Saints* her mother gave her when she married.

They are ready now, but they have to wait . . .

Around two there is a shout. Dominic, the Noonans' red-haired eldest boy, comes running up.

'They're coming!'

By the time the bailiff and the four emergency men reach the cottage, a small crowd has gathered in front of it. At the first sight of them the women have started up their din. Rose sees Lizzie Power and Annie Noonan banging spoons on kettles and the Duffy girls have tin cans strung about their arms and a big tin tray that Kathleen is banging with a ladle. Somebody has a foghorn – it is hard to see her face – and is blaring through it. 'Shame! Shame!' The angry yelling of the men is indistinct behind this word.

They all come out together, unresisting. Rose has pleaded with Michael not to be abusive; she knows of one tenant arrested and gaoled just for shouting 'God save Ireland!' when they dragged him struggling from his cabin.

Michael looks the bailiff in the eyes and the sting in his gaze meets the coldness of a man who is well enough used to being hated. For a moment the Tierneys stand frozen with the doorway at their backs, as if for a photograph to be taken, although none of them has ever faced a camera. Rose with Alfie shawled on her shoulder and holding Catherine tightly

by the hand, Elizabeth Anne clinging to her father's arm and
Gerald standing tall as he can make himself on Michael's other
side. Then, before stepping forward, Rose squints back into
the penumbra of the cottage and notices a poker forgotten by
the embers. Letting go of Catherine, in a quick movement she
turns and takes firm hold of it. Facing the light again, she sees
the men have stiffened. They retreat a pace or two, readying
themselves, gripping all the harder the crowbars and sledges in
their hands. The bailiff has a hatchet hanging loosely from his
arm, as if it belonged there. Rose becomes aware of how she
too might be wielding a weapon. Knuckles loosen as she
bends to pass the poker on to Catherine: 'Here, you carry this
for us.' Her voice is hoarse, as if there is grit in her throat. Her
face feels on fire.

'Come on, youse get moving!'

The words are deafening, bawled at them from just a yard
away. Alfie, quiet until now, opens his mouth and howls in
Rose's ear. Elizabeth Anne's low whimper turns to a sob and
Catherine blurts a plea of 'Mammy!' The Tierneys surrender
and advance into the arms of their clamorous neighbours.

Halfway through August and the blight has worsened. In
Fermanagh's poorer wetlands it is general, and in South
Tyrone. Cork fares badly, with tubers rotting already, though
in Limerick they say the disease is confined to the stalks.
Mayo is affected worst of all, with the crop almost entirely
destroyed. Galway, Waterford and Tipperary suffer sorely too.
Blight is widespread in North Kerry. This is fuel for 'agita-
tion', the landowners fear.

These fears grow daily, heightened by the widespread state

of inflammation they see among the lower orders. Telegrams requesting and guaranteeing solidarity criss-cross the Irish Sea, causing one Newry newspaper to demand 'a strong hand, in putting down the almost universal movement on the part of the working-classes to enforce their own arbitrary terms of labour, both as to time and money'.

The women in the Dundee jute mills pass a resolution for a wage increase. Postal workers go on strike, as do dockers in London and Dover and Ayr. The men in the London silk-hat trade return to work with demands satisfactorily met by the masters. Telegraph clerks win an overtime rate and extra for Sundays. Since the gas workers cut their hours from twelve down to eight, while raising their wages by sixpence a day, shorter hours has turned into a rallying-cry; loudest of all for railwaymen, whose working days can stretch to sixteen or seventeen hours. The General Railway Workers Union was founded just this year, born, like many others, from the turbulence of winter last.

Their South Wales strike draws other workers in their thousands on to Cardiff's streets. In the Saturday procession contingents file past from the National Amalgamated Labourers, the unions of carpenters and joiners, tinplatemen and rivermen, the shipwrights', seamen's and firemen's unions. There is mass support from the miners of the Rhondda. The miners intend to impede the passage of the company's trains.

When and where did it begin, this momentous advance of the masses, this erupting solidarity? Unions are no longer just for craftsmen, 'fossilised brothers' upholding special status, cherishing traditions. The matchgirls led the way in '88, in '89 the dockers showed that strength now lay in numbers. Brothers and sisters, skilled and unskilled, unite. All of these things were stirred by Bloody Sunday, when the perfect 100-acre plot of Trafalgar saw brutal battles rage on that November day in '87. That day too is 'How the Change Came' in William Morris's soothing fantasy of backwards progress into rustic calm where sweet, soft-robed women tend hearth and table. A world without cities. Yet how can change go backwards, when the Empire embraces five continents and speed pushes the earth's distant parts together towards modernity? Faster, faster, faster; with time itself in a new metabolism.

This is the summer that Cardinal Newman dies, *The Picture of Dorian Gray* appears amid scandalised protest, Adelina Patti sings the praises of Pears soap.

F stands for freedom, which old England brags about.
If you haven't got a dinner, why you're free to go without.

Sales of the People's Alphabet are doing a brisk trade in Hyde Park, together with ice-cold lemonade and nuts at a penny a mug. But most in demand are the thick spike-circled slices of pineapple, yellow like the sun bouncing off the brass of the trombones and trumpets, alighting on the many-coloured silks of the banners and leaving them resplendent. Rarely are banners unfurled without speeches, but this is no rally, and though the speeches are made hardly anyone listens, except when Ben Tillet and John Burns mount the podium.

Picture it, a labour picnic this August Sunday in 1890. Tillet inveighing against the 'hare-brained chatterers and magpies of Continental revolutionists', Burns good-humoured in a white straw hat. Young couples curled in the pools of deep shadow that the chestnut trees cast. A boisterous tide of people which ebbs and flows around the speakers and the vendors and musicians on the wide expanse of grass, happy with the confidence of the day, now that the century's hope in progress seems at last to be theirs to claim too.

Cissy makes tea for the Tierneys and they sit for a while, but the handcart is left unloaded. Then, before it gets dark, they set out with Joe along Hill Street towards the yard at Merchant's Quay. Cissy's two lodgers sleep in the kitchen, so there is no room for them there.

Rain is spitting down and the handcart skites and rattles on the cobblestones so roughly you can tell the loose wheel is nearly off. They stop and Michael tries to bang it in straight with the sole of his boot. Joe will fix it after, he says.

The coalyard shed is as clean as Joe could make it. He sometimes sleeps there when a shipment is due in the small hours, or his partner Patrick Sinclair does. They use it as their office, and faded yellow dockets hang on strings behind a dark nail-pitted door. Michael lights the oil lamp and Rose says the Hail Mary with the children, the three bigger ones kneeling down to pray before she tucks them up in their blankets. 'Matthew, Mark, Luke and John, bless the bed that I lie on . . .'

They wake early with the hurly-burly of the stevedores and carters just outside the yard and Rose goes out with a pail to get water from the pump on the canal bank. Michael sees to the brazier, and once they have had their tea and Rose has cut them each a slice of cold porridge from the slab she has wrapped for the journey, they wash their hands and faces in the bucket.

At half-past seven Joe comes to take them over to Bridge Street station. He has deliveries to make until eleven or later, so they have to go now, well in advance of the train. The children are happy up on the coal cart, with a piece of clean sacking slid under them. But riding through Newry like that, with the big plaid shawl wound round her again and Alfie huddled into it, Rose feels a pang of pure shame. Tears spring to her eyes for the first time since the moment yesterday when she turned and saw the shattered lintel of the cottage door, where the bailiff's men had made their mark.

The town has an early morning air of business as usual on this grey and clammy day and she cannot help her backward looks before they turn the corners, her eyes hooking on to random things: a street name, a public house sign, a man's checked suit swinging from a hanger slung over the awning rail of a shop; all these ordinary sights are separate and full, like components of a dream.

Later that day Newry's principal employers gather at the Athenaeum to discuss the volatile strike situation. The statement they issue is cautious, anticipating even greater ferment, foreseeing 'a general closure of concerns until such a time as a satisfactory arrangement could be come to between capital and labour'.

The Tierneys sail, not west but east. Waiting for them when they dock in Glasgow will be another Tierney, a cousin. He will help them find a home of sorts in one of the East End's tenements, and for Michael a job alongside him in the

Shettleston factory where sheep gut is converted into strings for tennis rackets. Rose will maybe take in sewing.

Glasgow is a great and prosperous industrial city, prospering all the more from the low wages paid to its workers, wages lower than those in England can expect, and lowest of all to the incoming Irish.

Northside, at the far end of the bridge, two high rows of letters climb into the sky. They are set atop a long contraption rising from the tallest of the rooftops. They are wider than the building underneath. Yet Rose cannot spell them into words. She squints and stares then turns to Michael to see if he can make them out. He shakes his head in puzzlement, but as they're jolted nearer he laughs and tells her that the writing's back to front, for reading from the other side. Because the city only starts across the river.

There it lies, just ahead of them, where all the drays and carts are trundling from the docks, with their loaded crates and sacks and barrels, and where they too are being driven on a double-decker tram as a pavement crowd streams past them towards the morning's work.

'What is it up there, Mammy?'

'Look, Catherine, you'll see it now: it's WILSON'S COLOS-SEUM.' The Tierneys point and gape, though dazed with tiredness from the day-and-night-long journey. They fill their eyes with new things; their ears are shocked by unaccustomed noise. Jamaica Street's thick press of traffic and its towering buildings soon enclose them.